PERSON

It was a sad shock for Holly when she heard of the deaths of her beloved grandparents. She had a much greater shock, though, when she found out how they had died and that the new laird, Calum McEwen, was laying claim to the cottage in the Scottish Highlands where they had spent their lives!

Books you will enjoy
by MARGARET MAYO

BRANDED

It was hardly surprising that Latham Elliot should hate her brother Carl, Susi thought ruefully, after the terrible thing that Carl had done to him. But for some reason it was hardly likely that Latham would think kindly of her, was it—let alone return her love for him?

DEVIL'S FANCY

It hadn't been Fiona who had embezzled from Brandon Rivers' firm but her identical twin sister Faith—but she couldn't manage to convince him of her innocence, and he proceeded to drag her off to the Bahamas to carry out his revenge. And then Fiona realised she was falling in love with him . . .

THE MARRIAGE GAME

Only three months after their marriage, Miranda's husband Georgios had hurried back to Greece, giving 'family troubles' as his reason—and he had not come back. So Miranda went out to look for him—and found that the 'family troubles' centred on Georgios' stern brother Theo, who refused to believe that they had been married at all . . .

RETURN A STRANGER

In the eight years since Lucas Delgado had jilted her on the eve of their elopement, Alina had never forgotten him—and when he suddenly turned up again she realised that she had never stopped loving him either. But if she had entertained any hopes of a reconciliation, those hopes were dashed for ever when the lovely Vanessa appeared on the scene!

PERSONAL VENDETTA

BY

MARGARET MAYO

MILLS & BOON LIMITED
15–16 BROOK'S MEWS
LONDON W1A 1DR

First published 1984
Australian copyright 1984
Philippine copyright 1984
This edition 1984

ISBN 0 263 74837 5

Set in Monophoto Plantin 10 on 11½ pt.
01–1184 – 53648

Made and printed in Great Britain by
Richard Clay (The Chaucer Press) Ltd,
Bungay, Suffolk

CHAPTER ONE

HOLLY had the strangest feeling that she was being watched. A peculiar sensation caused the hairs on the back of her neck to stiffen, yet when she turned there was no one to be seen; nothing except woodland and rolling hills sloping down to the expanse of shiny blue water.

Nowhere on earth, she was sure, could you find a place so peaceful and serene. The silence hurt your ears. She recalled as a child thinking that it was like living in a big glass dome and that if she threw a brick hard enough and high enough it would burst the bubble and she would hear the noise of traffic and of people.

Her summer holidays here had been a taste of freedom after being in prison. She could run and shout and do whatever she liked without fear of being a nuisance. There was no comparison between this sleepy Scottish glen and her home town of Walsall in the heart of the industrial Midlands.

But never had she felt she was being spied upon, of unseeing eyes watching her every move, of being—resented, a stranger not welcome in this private place.

'Holly Burns, you're being fanciful,' she told herself sternly. 'Simply because you've not been back for ten years there's no reason to feel that you're an intruder. You've as much right here as anyone, and don't you forget it.'

She firmed her shoulders and took a deep breath of

air filled with the smell of heather and peat, of pine and sheer clean freshness, and trod again the winding path along the glen to Braeside.

Very nearly she felt glad that her car had run out of petrol, otherwise she would have missed this first real taste and smell of the Scottish Highlands. On the other hand she would not have experienced this sensation of being unwelcome.

She had been so eager to reach her destination, so sure she would have enough petrol to take her these last miles that she had sailed past the last filling station, intending to fill up at Invercray in the morning.

Her little car stood now at the entrance to Glen Shilda, its flame red paintwork just visible through an avenue of lime and sweet chestnut, the colour totally at variance with the muted greens and purples of her surroundings.

Away to her left stretched a dyke and she followed the line of it up the hillside with her eye, remembering how her grandfather had told her that a dyker's skill lay in the knowledge of the laws of gravity, using the strength of overlapping joints and the natural fit and grip of rough rocks without the use of mortar.

This particular dyke denoted the boundary of her grandparents' property and it meant that round the next bend she would come upon the cottage.

A movement caught her eye and for a brief second a horse and rider were silhouetted against the skyline. They had been standing unseen against the wall, but now were distinctly visible and although they were too far away for her to see whether the rider was looking in her direction, she knew without a shadow of a doubt that this was the person who had been watching her progress—and whoever he was, he did not want her here. It was a man, she knew instinctively. No woman would sit so tall in the saddle, or control that magnificent animal so easily. Knowing she was being observed gave Holly an odd feeling and she could not rid from her mind the unease this unknown person caused.

As she stood the horse galloped along the ridge, the rider at one with the beast, the drumming of hooves now disturbing the silence that was so much a part of this glen.

Holly watched until they disappeared from view then trudged the last few yards to her grandparents' cottage—no—her cottage! It was hers now, she kept forgetting that. It would be strange going inside without seeing them.

Her mother hated this place. On her one and only visit prior to their marriage, before electricity came to the glen and there was no hot water unless you boiled a kettle or a saucepan on the fire, she had declared it uncivilised, and shuddered in distaste every time it was mentioned.

Consequently, when it came to school holidays, Holly's father brought her to his parents' cottage, but because it meant leaving her mother alone, never stayed more than a day himself. She was only nine when he was killed in an accident at the factory where he worked, and Holly's mother refused to let her visit her grandparents again. She complained that she was always wild and uncontrollable after these holidays, and that it was in her own interests that she stay away.

Naturally her grandparents were upset, and never

forgave their daughter-in-law for depriving them of seeing her. They wrote to Holly at Christmas and on her birthday, sending presents and home made sweets, but still Holly was never allowed to go.

When her mother remarried, Holly resented the man who took her father's place, and this feeling grew to hatred when he sided with her mother about the visits to Scotland.

Over the years, though, her memories of both her grandparents and their tiny but comfortable cottage faded, and when her mother passed on the news that they had died she was saddened but not devastated, accepting it as inevitable; ashamed, though, that she had not taken the trouble to visit them once she was old enough to lead a life of her own.

Perhaps if it had not been for Steve she might have done. But she had never wanted to leave him, always afraid that he might fall for someone else during her absence.

Steve had not wanted her to come now. 'It can be settled through the solicitor,' he had argued. 'What's the point in going all that way when you're going to sell?'

'I want to see it again,' she said stubbornly, pouting her full lips and flashing her green eyes.

It had been a surprise, discovering they had left it to her, although it should not have been since she was their only blood relative. But ten years was a long time. She had grown from a child to a woman and they, poor dears, had been denied the pleasure of seeing her grow up.

'If you wait until my holidays,' he said, 'I will come with you.' But Holly did not want to wait. It was true she had no intention of holding on to the cottage, but it would be nice to have a few keepsakes to remind her of her grandparents.

Thinking of Steve made her hasten her footsteps, effectively taking her mind off the unknown horse rider, and within seconds she could see the tiny cottage.

It was almost hidden behind a protective shield of colourful shrubs and trees and so vivid were her recollections that she almost expected to see a curl of smoke from the chimney and her grandmother waiting on the doorstep to welcome her.

Instead it stood cold and still and much smaller than she remembered. The windows were dull instead of sparkling as they always had in Granny's day. The garden untended, as though Grandad had not given it too much attention before he died.

But she was forgetting they were old. Granny was forty when her father was born. They had given up hope of having children. They would be over eighty now. They had had a good life, saddened only by the death of their son and their daughter-in-law's refusal to let them see their one and only grandchild.

Holly suddenly realised it was almost dark. It had taken her longer than she expected to get here and dusk had fallen so quickly it had taken her by surprise. She searched in her bag for the key that she had stopped at the solicitor's in Glasgow to collect, frowning in annoyance when it would not fit.

She cursed them for giving her the wrong one, then looking more closely at the lock realised that it was new and shiny. Someone had changed it!

Unbidden came to mind a picture of the horse and rider, then she dismissed this as mere fantasy. She had no reason to believe that he should do this to her.

Perhaps her grandfather had changed the lock before he died and the solicitor had unfortunately got hold of the wrong key? There could be any number of solutions and none of them need concern the man on the horse.

She went round to the kitchen door pushing back rambling roses that had started to take over, but the key did not fit here either, and she stood for a moment debating what to do next.

Had she not been so stupid as to run out of petrol she could have gone on into Invercray and found lodgings there, now she had no choice but to break a window and get in that way.

She knew there were no other houses in the glen, only the castle far away at the other end. It was not really a castle. It was a very large house belonging to the McEwens who had sold her grandfather this cottage and piece of land. The old Laird had come to Braeside once when she was there and he had had a row with her grandfather and she had felt the ground rumble, so deep and loud was his voice. He had a red face, penetrating black eyes and a bristling white moustache and she had never forgotten that day. She still felt slightly in awe of the McEwen family, and would certainly never dream of going to them for help.

It was amazing how guilty she felt, breaking a window in her own cottage. She felt like a criminal as she raised the brick, looking furtively over her shoulder in case anyone was watching.

The windows were so tiny that she had to break some of the framework before she had a hole big enough to climb in, not that it was hard work because the timber was old and rotten and whoever bought the place would need to replace it anyway. In effect she was doing them a favour, because tomorrow she would get a man out here to put in a new frame and find her a key for the lock.

Inside it was dark and cold and when she tried the light switches nothing happened, which wasn't surprising because with no one living here the electricity would be turned off.

She glanced about her in what little light there was left and her vague memories of gleaming brass and fresh cut flowers, of bread toasted before an open fire, eaten with the butter running down her chin, were soon dissipated.

Nothing was so cheerless as a house that had stood empty, she discovered. She was tired and hungry and did not know what it was she had expected but it was certainly not this. She should have known when she got up late this morning that nothing would go right. A puncture on the motorway had not helped. The day had been a disaster before she reached here.

But Holly was not one to let things get her down and before long she had a fire burning in the grate and a kettle of water singing on the edge of the hob. She thanked her grandmother for not getting rid of her black-leaded fireplace.

She pinned a sheet of brown paper over the broken window and drew the curtains across it, and found candles in a drawer which she stood in saucers and lit. She drank black coffee and ate biscuits and cold rice pudding out of a tin, and she filled a hot water bottle and put it in the bed she had slept in as a child. The sheets were clean and smooth and she had no qualms at all about sleeping in them.

It was a novelty going to bed by candlelight, watching her grotesque shadow on the wall as she undressed and pulled on her nightie, then sliding between cool sheets with their single patch of warmth where the bottle had lain.

She blew out the candle and lay in the darkness, completely unafraid in this house that had been her grandparents', which had been her father's home when he was a boy, and now belonged to her. Even though she had been away all these years there was a familiarity about it, it closed about her and protected her, and she would be a little bit sad when it was sold.

Not that there was any chance of her changing her mind. There was simply no point in keeping it when she would never live here. Steve, she hoped, would soon ask her to marry him, and he would not move here where there was no work. Besides, the money would come in very useful setting them up with a house of their own. They would have a better start than most. Something new and modern on an estate, that was what Steve wanted, and because she loved him it was what she wanted too.

Reaching out she pulled back the curtains and silver moonlight flooded the tiny room with its rag rugs and patchwork quilt, both lovingly made by Granny whose hands had never been still. An owl hooted but it was the only sound and very soon she fell asleep.

Holly was awakened by the sound of someone turning a key downstairs. It was daylight and the sun was quite high in the sky, but she had no idea what time it was. She sat up and listened then slipped out of bed and shrugged into a well-worn housecoat, belting it as she tip-toed down the enclosed stairs. She had left the door at the bottom open and across the room could see a pair of black leather booted legs, and lean powerful thighs clad in black jodhpurs. The feet stood slightly apart and whoever he was he was waiting for her.

Holly's heart pitter-pattered inside her breast and her mouth felt dry, her palms moist, and she knew instinctively that it was the man who had watched her arrival from the brow of the hill.

With each step she descended she could see more of him, narrow hips and the skirt of a dark tweed riding jacket; a crop sprung like a bow between lean, tanned, long-fingered hands, a broad chest with a thin black roll-necked sweater fitting snugly beneath the immaculate coat.

The firm thrust of jaw, the aggression in the set of the chin, made Holly slow down and stop before she saw the whole of his face. She sensed that here was an adversary. She might not know him, and he certainly did not know her, but that did not stop him from resenting her presence.

The atmosphere in that tiny room was such that she felt she could cut it with a knife.

It would choke her to walk into it, to face up to this man who was here for a reason known only to himself. That whip in his hand, she got the impression that he would like to use it on her, that he would derive much pleasure out of seeing her at his feet begging for mercy.

Yet he had said nothing. He had done nothing. As yet he was a faceless person and she was a prey only to her own over-fertile imagination. She ran a hand through the short curls of her auburn hair and realised that she was trembling.

Then she took herself to task for being stupid. She was in her own cottage. She, if anyone, was boss here. It was this man who was in the wrong. She took a deep breath, lifted her chin and stepped down the last two stairs.

She opened her mouth to ask who the devil he thought he was entering her cottage, but the words died on her lips when she looked into a pair of the coldest, unfriendliest dark eyes she had ever seen.

Her mouth remained open as she took in the uncompromising face that topped that powerful body. His lips thinned in a straight grim line, a hawk-like nose was bridged by strong brows over those piercing eyes. Thick, shining black hair waved about a well shaped head. He looked sinister and menacing and Holly involuntarily stepped back a pace, clutching her dressing gown tightly across her breast, feeling somehow naked and defenceless against this hostile stranger.

Later she wondered why she had let him speak first, but at that moment her mouth felt dry and contracted and in the long silence when they weighed each other up, which lasted seconds but felt like minutes, she could not have spoken had she tried.

'You do realise that breaking and entering is a very serious offence?' His deep-timbred voice filled the room, bouncing off the low-beamed ceiling and sending tiny quivers down Holly's spine.

But his autocratic manner put her immediately on the defensive, determined not to let this man, whoever he was, get the better of her. He was at least twelve inches taller than herself, six foot three or four, she ventured to guess, and the fact that she had to look up made her even more ill-disposed toward him.

'In my own home?' Holly's voice gave away none of her aggression. It was all sweetness and innocence, her green eloquent eyes wide, her fine brows arched with just the right degree of perplexity. Her cheeks still held the flush of sleep, her auburn curls framed her face in charming disarray.

But the man in black was in no way enchanted by the young girl who stood with apparent meekness before him. His brows jutted over those stone-cold eyes which eyed her insolently, probed the fine woollen material of the gown which covered a slender but shapely body. 'In *my* house,' he returned, the merest trace of a Scottish brogue softening the hard words. 'Braeside belongs to me, and if you don't get out immediately I shall have no compunction about throwing you out.'

These were the very words Holly needed to fire her temper. She lifted her chin in a characteristic gesture of defiance, much as she had used to her parents when as a child she could not get her own way, her eyes flashing with a brilliance that brought life to her face.

'I don't know who you are,' she said, 'but you would be wise to get your facts right before making such a statement. This cottage belonged to my grandparents, and now it belongs to me. So it is in fact you who are the trespasser, and if you don't get out, then I shall——' Her voice tailed as she had a quick mental picture of herself trying to lift this giant of a man.

His lips quirked, evidently the same thought occurring to him. He flexed the crop between his thumbs and fingers and Holly quite unconsciously touched her throat, imagining all too vividly those long lethal fingers snapping the slim column of her neck.

'You would . . . what?'

The suggestion of humour incensed her. 'I shall order you out,' she declared strongly, 'and fetch the police if you refuse to go.' She was trembling and furious with herself for letting this man rile her. 'I had a long journey yesterday, and you've just woken me up, and I'm not in the best of moods. Please go. You have no right here.'

'Since I have the key wouldn't you say that gives me every right?'

'So do I have a key,' snapped Holly. 'And it wasn't my fault that it did not fit.'

'In that case you should have turned round and gone back to wherever it was you came from.'

She eyed him coldly. 'Since my car has run out of petrol that would be impossible, and don't tell me you don't know, because you watched me arrive yesterday. If you were so dead set against me coming here why didn't you stop me then? Or do you make a habit of getting girls out of bed? Do you get your kicks out of threatening innocent females?'

Holly had never spoken to anyone so rudely in her life, and shuddered to think what her grandparents would have said if they could hear her. Good manners and politeness to strangers was a lesson she had had drilled into her many times. They would be appalled at the way she was speaking to this man now. But he deserved it. He was despicable. He had no right acting in this high-handed manner. Who the hell did he think he was?

His eyes narrowed at her barbed comments, nostrils flaring as he slapped his thigh with the whip. 'Damn it girl, you're going the right way to get molested.'

Holly jumped at the unexpected sharp crack of sound within the room and stepped back yet again. Her heel caught the bottom step of the stairs, knocking her off balance, causing her to fall heavily and ungraciously on her bottom.

Her faded pink gown fell open to reveal the entire length of her slender legs, her cotton nightie making her only just decent. His eyes, she noticed, were quick to observe her part nakedness but rather than let him see that his regard disturbed her Holly made no attempt to cover herself up.

Instead she rose slowly to her feet, allowing the gown to fall naturally to her ankles, thus hiding her legs which he had apparently found of interest.

It occurred to her that she could be in danger if she intimidated this man too much. There was no other living soul for miles. He could do whatever he liked and there would be no one to hear her cries for help.

But how could you be civil to a man who treated you like an intruder, who dared to suggest that this cottage was not your own? Holly shook her head angrily, setting her curls bobbing, and said, 'You lay one finger on me, mister, and there'll be big trouble.'

'Since it would be your word against mine,' he returned with maddening calmness, 'I hardly think you'd be the one to come out on top.'

She glanced at him haughtily. 'You carry some sway around here, eh? Is that what you're telling me? Well let me tell you that it makes no difference. I couldn't care less if you were royalty itself. I know my rights and if you touch me I'll cause the biggest uproar you've ever heard.'

Amazingly he smiled. 'Quite a firecracker for your size, aren't you? I must admit I admire a woman with spirit, but——' his smile faded, 'that does not mean I shall allow you to stay.'

Holly felt she was fighting a losing battle. 'I'm sorry, mister whoever you are, but we seem to be talking at cross purposes. I have proof that this cottage belongs to me.' Except that she had not brought the solicitor's letter with her! 'Have you?'

'The name's McEwen,' he said. 'Calum McEwen.'

Holly had a sudden vision of a white walrus moustache and another pair of equally fierce black eyes. She should have guessed. But the fear she had felt for the McEwen family changed abruptly to animosity. If this man thought he could lord it over her he had another think coming.

'The local landowner?' she asked haughtily. 'In that case you should know very well that your father, or was it your grandfather, sold my grandparents this cottage, and an acre of land to go with it.'

He looked at her with those eyes as cold as chips of black ice, his face as hard as the granite that tumbled in the burn a few yards from the door. 'Let's get the facts right, young lady. It was my great-grandfather.'

'Then you don't deny that he did sell this place?' pounced Holly eagerly.

'Not at all.' For the first time he put down the whip that he had toyed with ceaselessly since she first set eyes on him, glancing as he did so out of the window.

Holly followed his gaze and saw a magnificent black stallion cropping the grass outside. Its coat gleamed from a lifetime of thorough grooming, and muscles rippled silkily as he moved. Master and horse were well matched, she thought begrudgingly. Each a superb example of their species.

Physically, she supposed, he was the most exciting man she had ever met, and she would not have been human had she felt no sexual awareness. But so far as manners went, that was a different matter. He was insufferably rude, believing he only had to say the word and she would obey. Except that if he thought he had the power to subjugate her, then he was very wrong. No one walked over Holly Burns. She did not have her red hair for nothing—even if it was only very slightly red!

'So what right have you to say that it does not belong to me now?' There was only one thing wrong with this argument—she wished she was more suitably clad! Otherwise she was quite enjoying trying to get the better of this local laird who quite clearly thought that he had an open and shut case.

He smiled, but it held malice, not pleasure, his even white teeth bared like a savage dog's. 'My great-grandfather sold Alasdair Burns this cottage, but my grandfather, James McEwen, a keen betting man, from all accounts, won it from him over a game of poker.'

'You're lying!' Holly felt the blood drain from her face, and although she had expressed disbelief, there was something in the way he said it that made her feel he might be telling the truth.

'It is a fact,' he said, 'and if I were you I would sit down before you fall down, and close your mouth if you don't want to catch flies.' As he spoke he pushed a wheel-backed chair towards her, its padded cushion covered in chintz to match the covers on the armchairs by the fireplace. They were all her grandmother's work. This cottage had been furnished and looked after with loving care, it was their pride and joy, and now this hateful man was saying it had not been theirs for a long time, that it had reverted back to the McEwen family.

She snapped her teeth determinedly and although it went against the grain to accept the seat he offered she knew her legs would not hold her up much longer.

'If that were true,' she said tightly, 'why would it have come to me in my grandfather's will? He would have changed it. It must be you who's got it wrong.' But she only had to recall the argument between her grandfather and James McEwen to realise there could be something in what he said. She had every right to fear that man—and now here was a younger version doing his very best to intimidate her. 'It's probably all hearsay,' she said loudly and firmly, 'and until you can show me proof of this—ridiculous wager—I shall remain here.'

She realised this was a very rash statement to make, and completely in antithesis to her plans. She had intended nothing more than a thorough look around before selecting a few keepsakes, and then putting the place on the market. She had had no intention at all of living here for even a short length of time. One night and that would have been enough for what she wanted to do.

It was amazing how this man had made her change her mind.

A polished leather toe cap tapped impatiently on the floor and because she was reluctant to look up into his face Holly watched the long fingers that curled and uncurled at his side. 'You are doubting the word of a McEwen?' He made it sound as though this was unheard of.

'I am saying that I want to see it in writing,' she declared boldly. 'And don't forget I know my grandfather's handwriting, so please don't try to trick me.'

'Have you never heard of a gentleman's agreement?'

Holly looked up to see the thick brows knitted crossly, the black eyes fixed on her with an intensity that made her shrink back in her seat. But bravely she held his gaze. 'From what I hear your grandfather was no gentleman—it apparently runs in the family.'

Her intended insult was not missed. He drew in a sharp breath and took a half pace towards her. 'If I was not a gentleman I would put you over my knee right now, so think yourself lucky, young lady. As it is, I can think of a much more effective way of punishing you.'

Before she had time to wonder at this statement he hauled her to her feet, his hard fingers digging painfully into the soft flesh of her upper arms. With a suddenness that knocked the breath out of her body he pulled her against the solid wall of his chest, his arms clamped like iron bars about her back.

'What are you doing?' she hissed savagely, struggling to free her chin and looking into the blazing madness of his eyes.

A sneer curled the corner of his lip even as he lowered his head. With her arms pinned to her side there was no escape and Holly had no recourse but to watch that granite face loom nearer.

The touch of his mouth drew a strangled cry from the back of her throat and too late she struggled to escape. But then the urgent passion of his kiss awoke in her a response that was entirely unexpected. There was none of Steve's gentleness here, instead a powerful expertise that knew exactly what sort of a reaction he would evoke.

And—damn him—she felt as though the blood was draining from her. Her heart thumped with wild ecstasy, her pulses worked overtime. If he let her go she would collapse, that was a sure thing. She was drowning in a whirlpool of desire and sensation such as she had never experienced before.

CHAPTER TWO

IT took every ounce of Holly's will-power to stop herself from responding to Calum McEwen's kiss, and when he savagely put her from him she trembled and fell with relief on to the chair from which he had so mercilessly yanked her.

Although the embrace had been intended as punishment the few seconds spent in his arms had left her shaken and confused, and more excited than she had ever been in her life. He was undoubtedly a most aggressively masculine man, the tough uncompromising angles of his face adding to his attractiveness.

But that did not mean that she liked him any the more. Simply because he had drawn attention to his own sensuality, and she, fool that she was, had felt an immediate response, it changed nothing. In fact she despised him more now than she had in the beginning.

'A pity,' he said damningly, 'that you're a frigid little thing. I had thought with a temper like that——'

'I'd respond eagerly to your sexual advances, and in no time at all would be doing whatever you asked?' cut in Holly acidly. 'You've picked the wrong girl for that, Mr McEwen, and I'd thank you to keep your hands off me.'

The narrowed hardening of his eyes pleased her. It must surely mean that her insult had hurt. But she was unprepared for his next thrust.

'An unfortunate choice of phrase, Miss—er, Burns, is it? No one ever speaks to a McEwen like that and gets away with it. I'll give you just two hours to get out of here. I'll even help. While you're getting ready I'll fetch petrol for your car.'

Holly could never remember this room feeling so claustrophobic. Even with both her grandparents and herself here she had never been aware that there was so little space, so little air to breathe. This dominating male filled every corner, making her dizzy and breathless and not half so confident as she tried to make out.

Nevertheless she looked at him disdainfully. 'Thanks for nothing, and you'll be wasting your time because I'm not going anywhere. I like it here. I think I might stay for quite some time.'

No need to tell him that she was due back at her job tomorrow. Men like Calum McEwen needed taking down a peg or two.

'We'll see about that.' The mobile lips were clamped so as to be almost invisible, the flint-like eyes fixed firmly on her face. They were incredibly dark, so dark that the pupils were invisible, lost in their inky surroundings. In contrast the whites looked extra brilliant and his thick lashes framed them dramatically.

Although Holly wanted to look away such was the magnetic power of this man that she found her eyes locked into his in silent battle. She rose from the chair and unconsciously clutched her wrap more tightly about her. 'The only way, Mr McEwen, that you'll get rid of me,' she said slowly, her voice sounding oddly unlike her own, 'is by using force, and since you've *tried* to assure me that you're a gentleman, I don't think you'd do that.'

Her stomach felt as though it was tied into knots

and she was aware of a pulse flickering rapidly at the base of her throat. She lifted her hand to cover it, but not before those perceptive eyes had spotted the tell-tale sign.

A slow smile widened his lips, but there was no matching humour in the dark eyes. 'A battle of wills, Miss Burns? Good, I shall enjoy that. It sometimes gets a little—quiet—around here.'

'Maybe because no one else has the temerity to disobey you, *sir*.' There was a wicked glint in her eyes as she added this last word. 'But I have no qualms. This is not McEwen property, I don't care what you say. And if I've got to fight you for it, then I shall; whether it is a clean or dirty fight depends on you.'

'You've got guts for a mere woman,' he admitted ungraciously, 'and since you've thrown down the gauntlet it would be very cowardly not to take up the challenge.'

And this man was no coward. She had only to look at his inherent strength, his air of unyielding power, to realise that she had a fight on her hands. But she was no coward either. So it promised to be an interesting experience.

It was not until he had gone, pivoting on his heel and marching straight-backed from the room, that she realised that only once in all of this had she thought of Steve.

He would not be pleased if he knew she had entertained a man here in her nightie. Entertained! Put up with, hurled abuse at, that was more like it. It had been a revelation, meeting the local laird, but if he thought he was going to cheat her out of her rightful inheritance he was sadly mistaken.

She was not one of his, yes sir, no sir, three bags full

sir, employees, or tenants, or whoever it was he had dealings with. He looked like a man accustomed to authority, a man who always had his own way. A smile curved her lips. She, too, would enjoy a battle of wills.

Not for nothing was she the granddaughter of Alasdair Burns. His mild manner had been deceptive, beneath it raged a fiery temper and although she had not known he was a man to wage a bet, she was not altogether surprised.

He had always been careful to hold his tongue in front of the *wee bairn*, as her grandmother referred to her, but more than once behind closed doors she had heard her grandmother bearing the brunt of his violent moods.

On the other hand, she felt quite sure that if he had lost the cottage in such a manner he would have ensured that his will was altered accordingly. He was a stickler for keeping records straight. He liked everything down in black and white to such an extent that he made his wife keep an exact account of her housekeeping expenditure.

Holly could vividly recall helping her grandmother with these accounts, laboriously filling in the words and figures in her own immature handwriting, not realising at the time that in her own cunning way the woman was helping her with her maths.

But it was Steve she was supposed to be thinking about. What would he say about this mix-up? He had thought it a waste of time coming here, could not understand her need to make such a sentimental journey.

Although she was aware that she had shamefully neglected her grandparents during these last years when she had been old enough to make the journey on her own, it did not mean that she had not still loved them, or this cottage. It held many memories and she had not liked to think that she might never see it again.

Steve had no idea what it looked like, or even how isolated it was. He had never been to Scotland and could not imagine how the wild splendour of mountain passes, of countless lochs and singing burns, of an endless supply of good fresh air mixed with the smell of heather and the sea, could get through to you.

He would not know what to do with himself. Walking was an unheard of pastime so far as he was concerned, as too was fishing. His car took him everywhere, to work, to the pub, to the cinema. There was nothing like that here. He would hate it, that was for sure.

But to Holly it was all she remembered. She had carried a romantic picture round in her head and it had not let her down. Everything seemed smaller, naturally, it always did when you grew up, but essentially nothing had changed.

And she was certainly not going to let Calum McEwen spoil her pleasure. She wanted to get washed and dressed and go out and explore. She wanted to say to hell with you, this is my home, I like it and I'm staying, and there is nothing you can do about it.

The trouble was—if she went out—she would probably not be able to get back in. Knowing the laird he would barricade all the windows in her absence and mount an armed guard into the bargain.

She smiled at her own thoughts and suddenly full of life ran through to the tiny bathroom her grandparents had had built on to the kitchen. There was no hot water so she made do with a quick splash and feeling refreshed sped back upstairs and pulled on jeans that hugged her as if they had been tailor-made for her slender curves, and a thick arran sweater that she had knitted herself.

She ran a brush quickly through her untameable crop of curls and left her face bare. Who wore make-up in a place like this? She felt clean—and good—her friction with Calum McEwen having sharpened her wits, leaving her raring to go.

Food, she thought achingly, after she had made her bed and flung wide the window. But she stood a moment looking at the incredible beauty of her surroundings.

She was accustomed to seeing nothing but houses and traffic, with a few trees to relieve the monotony. Here, the only scar was the pylons which carried electricity through the glen, and the only movement that of birds in flight. She listened to their various songs, distinguishing the raucous cry of a rook, the chattering of starlings, and the pink-pink of a chaffinch. It was like a full-sized orchestra being played for her benefit.

The silver-blue water of the loch lapped gently against the rocky grey shore, and on the far side trees clung tenaciously to the sloping sides of Beinn Liath. The farther away she looked the more indistinct it became, hills losing their identity, becoming nothing more than purple mounds disappearing into a hazy sky.

Overhead, though, the sky was azure, the sun beaming down, turning this tiny Scottish glen into paradise on earth. Holly took a few deep breaths of the sweetly-scented air, enough to tell her that she was desperately hungry and that she really ought to get something inside her before the next confrontation with the arrogant man in black.

A bowl of porridge, yes, that was what she would have, good and thick like granny used to make. But the fire had gone out and by the time she re-lit it and boiled water there would not be much left of her two hours' grace.

So she ate cold baked beans and a couple of crackers washed down with a glass of water. Not exactly the most appetising of breakfasts, but it cured her hunger, if it did not exactly put her in the best of moods.

Really she needed to shop, but how could she without losing her questionable advantage? Perhaps Calum McEwen would have a change of heart when he realised how determined she was? Or perhaps pigs would fly! That man had no heart. You only had to look at him to see that it was carved out of stone.

She decided to do an inventory of what there was, and then if she needed to barricade herself in she would be able to ration out the food to last the longest time possible.

Really it was quite fun. The kitchen table was soon piled with tins and packets and her nimble brain was working out the best way to adapt the food to give her a varied and not too boring diet.

But it was what she found in a cupboard under the sink that excited her most. A door lock! A used door lock, but not rusty or broken. If her guess was right she could be in luck.

She fetched the key given to her by Mr Fraser, the solicitor, and tried it. Success! And Holly was no fool when it came to work about the house. Her mother was hopeless at anything practical, and her stepfather nearly as bad.

Holly had learned to decorate, to change plugs, fuses, washers, could use an electric drill and a saw, and was quite sure that something simple like changing one lock for another was not beyond her capabilities.

There was a gleeful smile on her face as she found a screwdriver and began to tackle the gleaming lock. It came off more easily than she had expected, and soon she had the other one in its place.

There was still the matter of the broken window frame, though. If she had climbed in that way so too could her adversary. Undaunted she searched what had once been an outside lavatory, later turned into her grandfather's storeroom for garden tools, etcetera.

She found a piece of plywood, a hammer and some nails, and by the time she heard the sound of her own car being driven quite recklessly and furiously along the track to the cottage she had it securely in place.

Pleased with her efforts Holly sat down in the most comfortable armchair the cottage boasted and prepared herself for his attack.

First of all he knocked on the door, when that failed to draw any response she heard his key in the lock, and then a roar of outrage as he realised what she had done.

'Miss Burns!'

She rather liked the way he rolled her name round his tongue.

'Open this door at once!'

'I don't have to,' she called. 'This is my cottage. Go away!'

There was a pause and then she heard him move round to the side of the cottage, testing the panel of wood she had fixed in place. It was then that she remembered she had not re-locked the back door. She had been so eager to get the work done before he got back that she had forgotten all about it.

They reached the door at the same time, and because he was bigger and stronger than she was he won. He stepped inside, a sadistic smile distorting his handsome face. 'You're not quite clever enough, Miss Burns. Ten out of ten for the do-it-yourself job, but for brains I guess you were at the end of the line when they handed those out.'

She looked at him coldly and refused to answer.

'Your car's waiting. And may I suggest that in future you keep an eye on the gauge? You might not find anyone else so willing to fill it up.'

'I didn't ask you to,' she snapped.

'Miss Burns,' he said impatiently, 'I am getting a little tired of all this. It's quite pathetic, you thinking you can get the better of me. Why don't you be sensible and take yourself off before things get ugly?'

Was it the black gear that made him look threatening, or was it all in her mind? It was quite dark in the kitchen, a holly bush that had been allowed to grow wild blocking out most of the light from the tiny window. With his face in shadow it was easy to imagine expressions that were not actually there.

There was no denying, though, that he was overpowering, that his six foot plus gave him a very definite advantage. She got the impression that if he so wished he could pick her up with one hand and deposit her wherever he liked. On the other hand there was still that sexual awareness that made sparring with him very exciting indeed.

Steve paled into insignificance beside him. Calum had that proud noble bearing of a Highland chieftain, accentuated by his aggression, making him a man above all men, a superior being. He was also rude and ill-mannered and clearly had no time for women. She detested him.

'I'm sorry,' she said, with as much dignity as she could muster, 'to keep labouring the point, but this is my property, and if things get out of hand it will be your fault. Why don't you just go and forget that I am here? I shan't be a nuisance, and I won't trespass on land that does not belong to me.'

He growled like a savage beast. 'You're missing the whole point, Miss Burns. I need this cottage. I have a new employee I wish to house here.'

'You should have made sure of your rights before promising it,' she returned sharply. 'You'll have to find him somewhere else.'

'It's not a him, it's a she, a lady, my new secretary,' he said impatiently. 'And she's arriving at the weekend.'

Holly eyed him sceptically. 'You're putting her here? So far away from your house? Why can't she sleep there if it's a resident secretary you require? There's plenty of room.'

His jaw firmed suddenly. 'Because I don't want her there.' There was something about the way he said it that made Holly look at him sharply. He sounded as though he hated women—yet he had kissed her! Why was that? Without thinking she touched her fingers to her lips, feeling again the hard bruising strength of his.

A quiver ran through her and she turned her head away as she saw the sudden gleam in his eyes. He knew what she was thinking! And that kiss had meant nothing. It had been a punishment, if one could call a kiss that. A retribution for her insults. Perhaps he had thought it would scare her, that she would run in case that one kiss led to something else.

But Holly was not afraid of men like Calum McEwen. He did not intimidate her, not in the slightest. If necessary she could look after herself. She had not taken lessons in judo for nothing. There were so many girls attacked and raped these days that she had felt it an essential part of her education.

Steve had thought she was mad. He was not a very physical person himself. He enjoyed a game of snooker or pool at the local pub, but that was about all, and he could not understand Holly's inexhaustible energy. She played squash and badminton, and loved swimming, although she did not have time to go to the local baths as often as she would have liked.

She eyed him disdainfully. 'You've left it rather late to get it ready. What were you going to do with my grandparents' things—chuck them out?'

He looked grim. 'It has been three months since the accident. I assumed no one was interested.'

'Accident?' Holly frowned strongly. 'What accident?'

'Really——' he began, but stopped when he saw her genuine confusion. 'You don't know?' His brows drew into a crisp straight line.

She shook her head. 'I haven't the slightest idea what you're talking about. Were my grandparents involved? But, no, they couldn't have been, my mother would have told me. You're having me on!' Her voice rose shrilly as she flung the accusation.

'I'm perfectly serious.' His face softened fractionally

as he took her arm. 'Let's go through into the other room. I think you ought to sit down.'

Holly shook herself free, glaring belligerently. 'Don't humour me. I'm tougher than I look. I shan't faint, or anything stupid like that. I want to know what happened—tell me—*now*!'

He sighed and took a deep breath. 'It's not pleasant, but since you asked, here it is. I really think you ought to sit down, though.' Again he attempted to touch her but Holly backed away, shaking her head, feeling the colour already beginning to drain from her cheeks.

'Your grandfather was cleaning his gun, he liked to do a bit of hunting, as I expect you know. Well, I suppose it's because he was old and a bit forgetful, he wasn't as careful as he should have been. The gun was loaded and——' He paused, seeming to have difficulty in finding the right words. 'He shot your grandmother.'

Holly gasped, putting her hands to her mouth in horror—and when Calum McEwen took her arm she let him lead her to a chair. Her heart clawed against her rib-cage and her eyes were full of tears as she looked up at him.

'It—it can't be,' she choked. 'You're making it up so that I'll leave here and never want to come back. That's it, isn't it?' She felt hysterical.

'I'm afraid not.' He shook his head, looking strained and upset himself. 'And there's more—where's your grandfather's whisky? I could do with a dram.' He disappeared into the sitting room coming back with a half bottle and two glasses. He poured them both one, handing Holly hers in silence, standing over her as she took her first sip.

He finished his own drink in one swallow and

poured another. 'Think you can take it?' It was surprising how gentle his voice had become.

She nodded and took another mouthful of the warming liquid which was setting fire to her icy bones.

'Alasdair was so—overcome—by what he had done—that he . . .' a long pause, 'turned the gun on himself.'

'Oh, no!' The glass fell from Holly's hands and shattered. 'Oh, God, no! Please tell me it's not true. *Please*, Mr McEwen.' She could not see him for tears but she felt the warmth of him as he gently pulled her to her feet and held her against him. She leaned her head on his chest and he smelt of horses and fresh Highland air, and he stroked her head gently, all the time murmuring words of comfort.

It was many minutes before she stopped shaking and sobbing, and Calum McEwen never once ceased to soothe and calm and hold her as though she was someone precious. She found it difficult to take in what he had said and she did not want to believe it, but it was such a cruel story that he would never have made it up.

When at length she became calmer he pressed a kiss to her brow and led her gently through into the other room. He sat her down on the couch, putting up her feet and covering her with a rug that had belonged to her grandmother. Then he poured her another glass of whisky and because her hands still shook he held it for her until she had drunk the lot.

Then he turned his attention to the grate, cleaning out the cold ashes and re-lighting a new fire. He washed his hands and when it was blazing sat down in one of the armchairs that was too small for his big body, and spoke for the first time since he had imparted his devastating news. 'How are you feeling?'

Holly smiled weakly. 'Better—I think.'

He grimaced. 'I'm sorry I had to do that. I really thought you knew. Someone should have told you.'

'Daddy's dead,' she said sadly. 'They were his parents.'

'And your mother? She must have been informed.'

'My mother never got on with her in-laws. Not that they thought much of her, although they were prepared to accept her for my father's sake. She was very beautiful—she still is. She sings in a night-club in Birmingham. She wears lots of make-up and dresses in tight clothes and——'

'You sound as though you don't like her very much?'

Holly shook her head. 'I don't. I think it all started when Daddy died and she wouldn't let me come up here any more. My grandparents were deeply hurt, I know, but I was only nine and had no say in the matter. My mother didn't even tell me they had died until after the funeral, and she never said—what had happened.'

'And you weren't close enough to her to ask?'

Her face contorted with pain. 'No, I wasn't. I thought they had died of old age. I thought that the shock of one of them going had caused the other to die of a broken heart.'

'Did you ever come to see them again, when you were older?

'No.' Holly looked guilty. 'You know how it is, you keep promising yourself but never seem to find the time. I wish I had.'

She wondered why she was opening her heart to this hateful man. Except that suddenly he was not hard and cold and unfriendly. There was a smear of coal dust on his nose and he looked human for the first time since she had met him.

'Has your mother remarried?'

Holly nodded. 'To another singer. I don't see much of them these days. They've got a flat in Birmingham near the club and rarely come home.'

'And where is home?'

'Walsall. I don't suppose you've heard of it. It's not far from Birmingham, about nine miles.'

'In the Black Country?' he grinned. 'A bit different from Scotland. Which do you prefer?'

She arched her fine brows. 'How can you ask? What can equal all this? Except that there's no work here. Steve would not dream of moving.'

'Steve? Is he your boyfriend?'

Holly smiled and nodded.

'Are you engaged?' He looked down at her slim bare hands resting on top of the crocheted blanket.

'Not yet.'

'But you're hoping to be?'

A dreamy expression crossed her face. 'It's only a matter of time.'

Calum McEwen moved so suddenly it startled her. His face changed, resuming its customary grimness, as though he had had enough of this conversation. He picked up the poker and attacked the fire viciously, throwing on a couple more logs, then standing with his back towards it, legs apart, hands linked behind him.

'What had you intended doing with this cottage—since your young man refuses to live here? Use it as a holiday home? Spend your honeymoon here, perhaps?'

There was something disparaging about the way he spoke that got Holly's back up. 'I think that is my business.'

'I think you should go back to your boyfriend,' he said. 'Now you've found out how your grandparents died it won't be pleasant for you here.'

'Is that why you told me?' she snapped.

'I told you because you asked,' he said with ill-concealed tolerance. 'But I know how a young girl's imagination can run away with her. I wouldn't advise another night spent here on your own.'

Holly swung her legs off the settee. 'I'm not frightened. You're not going to get rid of me that easily.'

'So how long are you staying?'

Did that mean he had given up trying to throw her out? wondered Holly. 'For as long as it takes to prove that I'm the true owner,' she answered without thinking, wondering what her boss would say if he could hear.

He had been reluctant to let her have a couple of days, even though they were owing her. 'Holly,' he had said, 'can't you wait until Sally comes back?'

Always they were too busy. She had helped him out often enough. If she had waited she would never have got them.

'Have you no job?' asked Calum McEwen abruptly.

'As a matter of fact, yes, but I'm on holiday—and until I met you I was really looking forward to a few days' peace and quiet,' she lied ebulliently.

Thick brows disappeared into dark hair. 'And your boy friend, he doesn't mind you taking off like this; a young attractive woman, alone, vulnerable? Anything could happen. If you were my woman I wouldn't let you go.'

If she were his woman! Holly found herself wondering what it would be like to belong to Calum

McEwen. She recalled the feel of his arms about her when she was upset. His strength had flowed into her, helping her, warming her. It had felt good. He was the sort of man who would protect his woman through thick and thin. If he loved it would be with a passion that would survive all odds. She would be a very lucky woman.

'But I'm not,' she said, 'thank goodness.' Now why had she added that after all the kind thoughts she had had about him? 'And Steve was naturally concerned but——'

'He couldn't stop you because you're a stubborn young thing,' he interjected bitterly. 'What sort of a man is he? He'll need to be strong to manage you.'

Holly stood up, her green eyes sparking antagonism. 'When I want your opinion I'll ask for it. Steve and I get on very well. He knows I can take care of myself.'

'Bully for him,' came the disparaging reply. 'But he didn't know you'd find the likes of me here. What would he think, I wonder, if he knew the two of us were alone in this cottage? Would he still think you were capable of coping?'

'With you?' It was Holly's turn to shoot her brows up. 'You don't intimidate me, Mr McEwen.' But he did make her pulse rate quicken and there was a definite sensualism in the long line of his body. He had shed his jacket when he lit the fire and the thin woollen sweater revealed a powerful phsyique that had been hidden beneath the riding jacket.

It seemed unfair that he should be so sexually attractive when he had a definite down on women. She wondered what had happened to make him feel like this.

'No, I don't believe I do,' he said, and he sounded surprised. 'In that case why don't you try calling me

Calum? It's much more friendly. And I shall call you——?' He waited expectantly.

'Holly,' she supplied tightly, reluctantly.

'Holly.' He repeated the name experimentally. 'Yes, I like it. It suits you. Nice to look at but needing careful handling. Very apt. Tell me, what sort of work is it that you do? You've a zest for living, I can see that, so I imagine it is something that uses a lot of energy.'

'I'm sorry to disappoint you,' she said drily. 'I'm a shorthand typist, a dull, boring, routine shorthand typist, who works for an equally dull and boring solicitor.'

'So why do you do it?'

She shrugged. 'It's a job, they're hard to come by these days. Sometimes I think I might scream at the monotony of typing another conveyance, but I don't have much choice.'

If he were her boss he wouldn't be boring, she thought. She wouldn't mind working for him. She could build up all sorts of fantasies about sexy Calum McEwen that she would never be able to do with dry-as-dust Mr Spindleton.

'How would you like to work for me?'

The question, following her own thoughts so closely, took her by surprise. She stared, open-mouthed, for a good few seconds. 'For you? You must be joking. I wouldn't work for you if you were the last man on earth. I don't trust you for a start, and I resent the way you're trying to kick me out of here. In fact I——'

'Hate my guts?' he cut in unsmilingly. 'I rather thought you did. But even so, the offer still stands. I'll double whatever wage it is you're earning now. When will you start, tomorrow?'

CHAPTER THREE

HOLLY looked wide-eyed at Calum McEwen. 'You're mad! How about the woman you've engaged? What would you do about her? Calmly write and tell her she was no longer wanted?'

'Something like that,' he shrugged, giving the impression that he did not really care.

There was no denying that the thought of working for this man was tempting. He had an aura of virility that was so strong it was overpowering. There was a primitive quality about him that drew out the basic woman in her, and no matter how she tried she could not resist.

She shook her head strongly, more to convince herself than him. 'I couldn't. It wouldn't be fair on Steve.' And it would be decidedly dangerous. He was far too attractive for her peace of mind.

He looked down at her from his great height. 'You would have your meals up at the house so you'd be able to save almost all of your salary. It would help, when you get married, it would give you a good start.'

'You sound pretty desperate,' she shot angrily. 'What happened to your last secretary? If you're really so generous I can't see why she should have left.'

'None of my secretaries last long,' he said coldly. 'I don't think I need go into the reason why.'

'I expect I can guess,' said Holly cuttingly. 'You can't keep your hands off them. What was wrong with the new secretary that you wanted to house her here?

Not your type, eh? An old spinster perhaps? I'm sorry, *Mr* McEwen, it's not my kind of job. I prefer a boss who keeps his hands to himself.'

'You little bitch,' he snarled, frightening her with his sudden ferocity. Up till now he had stood in front of the fire, looking very much at peace with the world. Now he sprang towards her, fixing his big hands on her shoulders, each finger digging painfully into her flesh.

'Let me go!' demanded Holly angrily.

'When I'm good and ready,' he grated. 'No one speaks like that to me and gets away with it. Just to keep the records straight I never force my attentions on any woman.'

'You're crazy if you expect me to believe that.' Holly eyed him hotly. 'You'd met me only ten minutes before you were—molesting me.'

His grip tightened as he listened to her harsh words, his thumbs sliding towards her windpipe until Holly was suddenly afraid for her own safety. She had never before had to use her judo training in self-defence but now she lifted her two hands, palms together, up between his arms, forcing them upwards with the suddenness of her movement. Then she swung her arms wide so that his own were thrown outwards.

In seconds she was free and although she could have followed through with a movement that would have rendered Calum helpless, she did not think the occasion called for such positive action. Nevertheless she stood poised and ready in case he came back at her.

Calum looked shocked, and then annoyed, and then amazingly he laughed. A deep rumble that came from somewhere low in his stomach and shook his whole frame. 'My God, girl, where did you learn to do that? So professionally as well.'

She shrugged and relaxed and looked suitably modest. 'A girl needs to be able to protect herself.'

'But a slip of a thing like you. I can see I shall have to watch myself. I'm glad I found out. What else can you do?'

'That would be telling,' she said with a quiet smile.

She liked it when he was on her side, when he wasn't aggressive and inhuman. It might even be a pleasure to work for him under those circumstances, but when he threw his weight around, when he assumed that because he had asked she would not dream of saying no, then she was very much against him and everything he stood for.

Still with that wide grin on his face he held out his hand. 'Shall we call a truce?'

Holly eyed him warily, not at all sure that this wasn't a trick, that he would not try to pull some move on her, catching her off guard as she had him. She wiped her hands down the leg of her jeans, pulling her jersey straight, before finally giving him the benefit of the doubt and putting her small hand into his.

His clasp was warm and firm and sent shivers through her that should never have been. She tried to look him in the eye but found her gaze sliding instead over the strong sweep of his jaw, the chiselled nose with nostrils flaring attractively. His skin was firm and tanned with a network of tiny almost invisible lines round his eyes. She guessed he was in his mid-thirties and he was different from any other man she had met.

'I'm glad you're being sensible.' His coal-black eyes smiled at her. 'Does it mean you'll come and work for me? Perhaps I'd better say please? It could prove painful antagonising such a dangerous lady.'

He was mocking her, yet at the same time Holly guessed this was the nearest he had ever got to pleading with anyone. Calum McEwen struck her as the sort who usually got his own way without having to ask twice.

And even before he had finished speaking she knew she was going to be another statistic. It was sheer madness, and Steve would be furious, not to mention Mr Spindleton, but she wanted to do it, she wanted to see more of this fatally attractive man whom she hated one minute and begrudgingly liked the next.

But more than that, she wanted to find out about this wager her grandfather was supposed to have made. There would be people at the house whom she could talk to, who would remember Alasdair Burns, who would know whether Calum was speaking the truth. For all she knew he could have made it up for her benefit.

'I'll think about it,' she compromised. 'I'll have to ring Steve, naturally, because he's expecting me back to—towards the end of the week.' She had almost said today. But that would have meant questions and admitting she had planned to sell. Now she was determined to hang on to the cottage at whatever cost. A fight with this man would be exhilarating.

He nodded and gave her her hand back. 'It's as good as settled then. You can come up to the house and use the phone.' He picked up his jacket and slid it over his broad shoulders. His dark hair was shaped around his ears but waved almost to his collar at the back. It was thick and wiry and Holly had an insane urge to feel its strength beneath her fingertips.

He settled the guard round the blazing fire and opened the front door, then turned to look at her still standing on the hearth. There was a hint of impatience in his voice. 'Are you waiting for something?'

'I don't like being rushed,' she said, trying to sound cool but still quivering from the after-effect of having held his hand so long. It was stupid to get in a tizz over such a small thing that had meant nothing to him, but which had turned her stomach upside down and left her feeling that she must be out of her mind. She needed a minute or two to pull herself together.

He folded his arms and leaned against the door jamb. His hair brushed the top and if he stood up straight he would hit his head. He said nothing but there was a look of intolerance on his face that warned her not to goad him too far.

'I'll just lock up,' she said, moving through into the kitchen and sliding the bolt. Then she picked up the key that fitted the lock she had returned to its rightful place and announced herself ready.

'You still don't trust me, do you?' he said, eyes narrowed speculatively. 'What do you think, that this is a trick to get you out of the cottage?'

She half shrugged. 'I wouldn't be surprised.'

'Let's say that I've discovered you're one very determined young lady, and that, amazing as this may sound, I admire you for it. I shan't lock you out again, Holly. For as long as you work for me you can use the cottage.'

Holly expelled her breath through gritted teeth and it took every ounce of self-control not to give him the answer he deserved. The cheek of it! No way was she going to accept that the cottage was his. For the moment, though, it suited her purpose to take this job. He could not imagine the satisfaction it would give her to prove herself right and him wrong.

He led the way to her car but she could not bear the thought of sitting so close, to have those long rangy legs stretched out beside her own, his arm brushing hers when he changed gear. A mini was no car for such a big man.

'I'd rather walk, if you don't mind,' she said. 'I could do with some fresh air.'

Surprise widened his eyes. 'It's two miles, are you forgetting? And you do have to come back.'

'Are you insinuating I'm incapable of walking that far?' asked Holly quickly. 'Or is it yourself you're thinking of?'

His lips quirked. 'I keep forgetting that you're much stronger than your size suggests. It's fine by me, let's go.'

For the first half a mile or so they walked in silence. Holly had forgotten how beautiful Glen Shilda was. They crossed a handsome stone bridge that spanned the river where it flowed into the loch, and paused a moment to look at the sun-kissed stretch of water with wooded hills sloping sharply down on each side.

Mallard, with their brilliant green heads, entertained them as they upended themselves in search of food. Little grebes chased after each other and silent swans glided majestically by.

It was so different from the busy grey town she had left behind that Holly could have dawdled there all day. Small white puffy clouds sailed in an azure sky, willow trees bending low over the water were fresh and green. It was the most peaceful place on earth.

Her eyes sparkled as she turned to the man by her side. 'I'd forgotten how incredibly beautiful it is. I wish I hadn't left it so long before coming back.'

'Or perhaps as a child your eyes weren't opened to

our wild Scottish beauty? Perhaps it took a few years living in a town to learn to appreciate nature in the raw.'

He could be right. She had taken it for granted when she spent her holidays here. She had never seen it with unblinkered eyes as she did now. 'Have *you* ever thought of living anywhere else?' she asked.

He shook his noble head. 'I've spent a lot of time abroad, a few years in London, but Shilda is my home. I'm here to stay now. My father died last year and the estate belongs to me. I intend looking after it to the best of my ability, improving where possible. As a matter of fact I have a new herd of pedigree cows coming tomorrow. The potential is quite staggering.'

'Are you married?' The question was out before she could stop herself.

'Heaven forbid!' he said strongly, straightening his back and resuming their walk across the bridge. 'I want no woman trying to change my way of life.'

Holly wondered why she felt disappointed, quickening her steps to catch up with him. He loped rather than strode, like a jungle animal, and she was almost running by the time she reached his side.

'But surely you want a son, to carry on your name?'

He shot her a caustic glance. 'My private life is my own affair. I'll thank you not to be impertinent.'

'I didn't mean to be,' she said, 'but it's not natural, is it? I mean, if Shilda means as much to you as you say, it's criminal not to plan for the future. You must have children. You need a wife.'

He stopped abruptly and faced her, his brow like thunder, almost matching the black clothes that he wore so superbly. 'You're not suggesting yourself for the part?' His narrowed eyes were hidden through the framework of thick lashes and the rapport she had felt a few minutes earlier disappeared.

Holly felt the blood rush to her cheeks, mortified that he had misinterpreted her words. 'Me? I wouldn't marry you if you got down on your knees and begged. I have Steve, don't forget.' Except that oddly Steve had faded into the background of her mind. This big, dark, most masculine of men was taking over her life, and her mind, and if she were not careful, her body. He was the most exciting male animal she had ever met, especially when he threatened her, like now. Her adrenalin flowed and her heart-beats quickened, and her eyes glowed like emeralds in her rosy face.

'Good!' he snapped. 'And in case you ever get any ideas about me, let me tell you here and now that I like to choose my own women. There are too many who think they know what is best for me. You're not the first to tell me I ought to get married, and each one has had an ulterior motive. Secretaries in particular seem prone to that sort of advice.'

It was an effort not to turn away from the cold menace in his eyes, but somehow she managed it. 'So that is why you were putting Miss Drummond in *my* cottage. Are you afraid of women, Mr McEwen? Can it be that a big handsome man like you does not know how to handle them?' She was flirting with danger and enjoying every second of it.

But even so she was not prepared for his physical attack, the suddenness of his hands on her arms, and when she tried to throw him off he was ready for her, countering it with a movement of his own.

'Touché, I think,' he said unsmilingly. 'Shall we continue our walk? You are wasting a lot of my time.'

So he was versed in the art too, thought Holly in

surprise, wondering why he had let her get away with defeating him on that first occasion. She felt a little bit ashamed of herself for goading him, and wondered whether she ought to apologise, or whether that would make matters worse.

In the event she kept quiet, walking a few paces behind him, some of her pleasure in their beautiful surroundings fading. Long before they reached Shilda House Calum was ahead. She had not bothered to keep up with his long-legged stride, and he had not deigned to shorten his steps to match hers.

From a distance it looked like a castle, built in mock-Gothic style more than two hundred years ago. As a child it had awed her with its magnificence, now it struck her as pretentious, far too big a house for one man to live in, especially as he had no inclination to get married and raise a family.

It was the first time, however, that she had seen it at such close quarters. It was situated high on the slopes of Beinn Liath, in such a position that the whole of the glen was visible from its windows. It was surrounded by a forest of oaks and birch and as she came out into the sunshine once again Holly gasped—and almost turned tail and ran.

If it had looked impressive from far away, it was overpowering standing beneath its sandstone walls. Yet it was not unwelcoming. Each pane of glass winked and smiled in the rays of the sun, and the brickwork, mellowed with age, looked warm and hospitable.

Calum had disappeared through ornamental iron gates and she walked hesitantly now over cobbles that were laced with moss, that looked pretty and decorative, but which, she felt sure, would be treacherous when the winter snows fell.

She paused in front of an immense arched door built out of solid oak, adorned with a black knocker in the shape of a fox's head. It stood open but she felt reluctant to enter, until Calum appeared and demanded whether she was going to wait there all day.

Her footsteps echoed on the marble-tiled floor as she followed him through the long hallway into a room that was darkly panelled yet with the clever use of pale furnishings managed to look light and airy.

It was a lived-in room with a fire burning brightly in the immense open stone fireplace, despite the fact that it was summer, and surprisingly great vases of roses which spilled their heady perfume into the room. There was a telephone on a table beneath one of the narrow windows which stretched grandly from floor to ceiling, and Calum indicated it now.

'I'll tell Hamilton you're staying for lunch while you make your call.' Without giving her the opportunity to argue he went out, closing the door firmly behind him.

It was not until she had dialled the number and received no reply that Holly realised Steve would be at work. It was strange how time had no meaning here. Back home she would have been dashing about trying to fit in a hundred and one jobs before the clock beat her, yet here it did not matter. You ate when you were hungry and went to bed when you were tired. It was as simple as that.

While she waited for Calum to return she studied a portrait over the fireplace of a gentleman in Highland dress. He stood proud and regal and had the same thick brows and black eyes as Calum. His nose was longer, his lips thinner, but there was no mistaking that he was a McEwen.

'James,' informed Calum when he came in and saw her looking at the picture.

'Your grandfather? The one who claims to have won Braeside over a lousy game of cards?' Holly was immediately on the defensive.

'The very same.' His mouth twisted wryly. 'Handsome beggar, don't you think?'

'Cruel,' answered Holly, noting the downward curve of his mouth, the cold hardness of the painted eyes. 'Ruthless. A penny-pinching Scot if ever there was one.'

He thrust his hands into the pockets of his breeches, turning away from his appraisal of the portrait and eyeing her coldly instead. 'Considering you profess to like Scotland you have a very poor opinion of its people.'

'When they rob old people why should I think otherwise? Except that I don't tar them all with the same brush. My grandparents were two of the most generous people you could find.'

And he was the most maddening—in more senses than one! He irritated her beyond words with his condescending, I am holier than thou, manner; she hated everything he stood for, but conversely he had an earthy animal-like magnetism. A formidable sensuousness that was so strong it threatened to choke her.

Even in this big room where there was plenty of space for her to get away from him, he took over. He filled every corner with his presence. It was stamped indelibly on each of the antiques that made the room what it was, on the tartan carpet which matched that of James McEwen's kilt.

She suddenly wondered what Calum would look like in a kilt. Very magnificent, she imagined. He had the height and breadth that would do Highland dress justice. With a sporran and belt, and a *skean dhu* tucked into one of his tartan socks, he would look very dashing indeed.

He chose not to rise to her gibe, saying instead, 'Lunch is ready when we are. Hamilton is laying another place. The guest bathroom is at the top of the stairs if you'd like to wash your hands. Oh, I almost forgot, how did your boyfriend take the news?'

Holly eyed him coolly. 'He wasn't in. I'd forgotten he'd be at work. I shall have to try again tonight.' She wondered whether she was doing the right thing, staying on to prove her ownership of the cottage. It meant giving up a good job, it also meant asking an awful lot of Steve. Although they were not engaged, and strictly speaking she was free to do whatever she liked, it seemed somehow disloyal.

Calum looked oddly pleased. 'Then you may as well wait here, and since there's so much work to be done you can start at once. My last secretary left two weeks ago and it's been chaos since.'

'I've not yet said I'll do it,' returned Holly heatedly. 'In any case I intend spending the time getting some supplies from Invercray—and I need to see about having the electricity put back on. There's a thousand and one jobs to be done.' Before he could answer she added quickly, 'Where did you say the bathroom was, upstairs?'

If the work had piled up it was his fault. He should have done it himself instead of wasting time riding, spying on newcomers and going out of his way to be unpleasant.

She left the room feeling bad-tempered and out of sorts, and matters were not made any better by the opulence of her surroundings. Her feet sank into a thick red carpet, each step she took cushioned in comfort.

Portraits of earlier McEwens lined the gallery, all with coal-black eyes, all equally arrogant and handsome, and cold and hard! The bathroom door was ajar and she went hurriedly inside, glad to shut out all those pairs of eyes which seemed to look at her with disapproval.

The room was warmed by a central heating radiator hidden behind an unobtrusive grille. She guessed that although the day was warm this was a cold house and needed heating almost all the year round.

The carpet was the colour of heather and the towels bracken green. It was a man's room with plain unscented soap and no fripperies, but the water was hot and the big bath tempted Holly after her sketchy wash that morning. But Calum had said lunch was ready. Hamilton, whoever he was, would not be pleased if she kept them waiting.

It was with apprehension that she joined him in the small room that was probably a breakfast room and commanded a view along the entire length of the glen. There was the river meandering its way along to the loch, which looked longer and wider from up here, its surface disturbed by a playful breeze. Highland cattle dotted green pasture and away in the distance a spiral of smoke from the cottage chimney—a tell-tale sign in itself. Even if he had not seen her arrival he would have come to investigate.

Hamilton turned out to be a dour individual with a long thin face and very little hair. He eyed Holly silently as Calum made the introductions and she was left with a feeling that here was one man who would not welcome her presence. Perhaps he too was a woman hater? Perhaps that was why Calum had picked him.

But it mattered little. She ate the delicious steak pie with its melt-in-the-mouth pastry, and wondered if the hostile Hamilton had made it. His looks were deceptive if he had.

'I enjoyed that,' she said when she had finished. 'Thank you.' They had eaten silently, Calum chewing his food at great length, deep in thought, miles away from Shilda House and his companion.

Now he brought his attention back to her. 'I'm glad. Hamilton is a good cook, and that is only a taste of the meals you will get. It will certainly save you having to cook for yourself. In point of fact there's no need for you to go shopping, and the electricity—well—it will be back on on Friday. It had been arranged in readiness for Miss Drummond. You can stay here until then.'

'You've changed your tune,' said Holly before she could stop herself.

His lips tugged down at the corners. 'I think that you and I, my little prickly friend, understand each other. I am quite sure that you will not—what shall I say—throw yourself at me?'

'You're right there,' she exclaimed, more loudly than she had intended, 'but I don't think it's a very good idea all the same. I wouldn't trust you an inch.'

Hamilton appeared in the doorway and it was evident by his pursed lips that he had heard. She guessed she had gone down another notch in his estimation, and it was now highly unlikely she would be able to get any information out of him.

He took away their empty plates and placed a very

filling-looking suet pudding in front of them. Holly felt this was winter food and wondered whether he ate as much himself as he expected them to do, but he was so thin and spare it could not be possible.

Calum helped himself to a generous portion, after she had shaken her head when he pushed the dish towards her, covering it with thick creamy custard and eating with the healthy appetite of a man who spends much of his time working out of doors.

It was not until they were drinking their coffee out of extra-large china cups, that he referred to her earlier heated statement. 'You'd be quite safe. I have no intention of seducing you. And besides, all the bedroom doors have bolts—on the inside—so if it is your wish you can shut yourself in.'

He watched her closely as he spoke, eyes dark and enigmatic over the rim of his cup, and she thought to herself, how can you shut anyone out mentally? Physically she felt in no danger, but the longer she spent in his company the more she realised she was attracted to him in a way she had never anticipated.

Steve was a nobody in comparison. An insignificant little man who meant nothing at all to her. And this was wrong. She loved Steve, she was expecting him to propose, she wanted him to. She wanted to spend the rest of her life with him. Or she had thought she did, until she met this domineering Scot who was turning her life upside down without even knowing it.

It was a strange feeling. She felt as though she was standing at the parting of the ways. One led her back to Steve, and sanity, and the calmly ordered life she had left behind. The other to Calum, to excitement and possible unhappiness, to a world where she would be sexually alive, but where there could be no fulfilment.

And once her mission here was finished would Steve want her back? It was a question she must ask herself. Would she want to go back? After her tussle over the cottage, whether she won or lost, would she be able to leave Scotland and live once again in busy Walsall where they made leather purses and saddles, where there were factories and foundries, and housing estates, and lots and lots of people—but no open spaces? No smell of heather and pine trees, no sense of freedom. Everyone living by the clock; getting up and going to work, coming back, watching television and going to bed, and then the same thing all over again the next day, and the next, for the rest of their lives.

'You're still unsure?' He looked amused. 'What can I say to make you believe that I'm not a big bad ogre?'

She looked into the clear purposeful eyes and suddenly made up her mind. 'Very well, I will stay.' But not for the reason that he thought, simply because she would be able to find out much more quickly about her grandfather's supposed wager. Hamilton would not talk, that was for sure, but there must be other staff. One man alone could not keep this mansion in such excellent order. If she actually lived here she would soon find opportunities to talk to them.

'Good!' He smiled warmly and reaching across the table took her hand. 'Welcome to Shilda House.'

It was with surprise that she noticed his eyes were not black after all, but a very dark velvet brown. She had seen them glittering as hard as pebbles, but at this moment they were warm and encompassing and sent quivers like quicksilver through her veins.

It occurred to her that this man, who inexplicably played havoc with her emotions, arousing feelings that she had never felt with Steve, could be the reason she wanted to stay. Not the cottage, not her outraged sense of injustice, but Calum McEwen himself.

CHAPTER FOUR

'HELLO, Steve.'

'Holly, you're back! I'll be right round. How did the trip go? It wasn't too much?'

Holly pulled a wry face at the telephone in her hand. 'I'm not back yet. I—I've decided to stay on for a little while.' The words came out in a rush.

'You're still in Scotland?' He sounded incredulous. 'But why, love? What fun will it be on your own? You've not changed your mind about selling? I knew it was fatal letting you go.'

She could imagine the frown on his face, a broad hand pushed through the tousled thatch of sandy hair. He would be wearing the brown cords he always had on in the evenings, and the check shirt she had bought him last Christmas. You could almost say they were his uniform, he wore them so often.

'There's a hitch,' she said, knowing she could tell him nothing short of the truth. 'I'm not so sure that the cottage belongs to me after all.'

'What do you mean? Is someone constesting the will?'

Holly shook her head, forgetting he could not see. 'Nothing like that. According to what I've been told my grandfather lost it over a game of poker. It's reverted back to the McEwen family. It used to be theirs before Grandad bought it.'

'You've seen proof of this?' he asked sharply.

'No,' said Holly. 'That's why I'm staying. It's word

of mouth only. The old man who made the bet is dead as well, but I'm going to ask around, and I shan't leave until I'm satisfied. No McEwen is going to do me out of what is rightfully mine.'

There was silence for a moment as Steve digested this piece of news. When he spoke he sounded worried. 'I admire your spirit, Holly, but is it really up to you? Why not leave it to your solicitor? You can't stay there indefinitely. How about your job?'

Holly grimaced. 'I was hoping you'd ring Mr Spindleton and tell him I won't be going back.'

'Not going back?' he echoed. 'For pity's sake, Holly, how long do you intend staying there? You won't get another job, you know that, not the way things are. And if we're going to——' He stopped and there was a long silence before he said quietly, 'get married, we'll need all the money we can get.'

Holly felt her jaw drop and she was glad Calum was not in the room at that moment. 'That's the strangest proposal a girl's ever had, Steve Kelly.' She endeavoured to keep her voice light, but it was difficult. Prior to coming here it was the one question she had waited for him to ask, now that the time had come she wished he had never mentioned it. Things had changed. In the space of thirty-six hours she had changed. She had met a man who had turned her world upside down. A man who was a sworn bachelor, who would never marry her no matter what, but who had made her realise that marriage to Steve was not what she wanted at all.

Steve was your average man. Of medium height and build, with a pleasant disposition, liking his pint in the pub with the boys, not always thoughtful, but kind and steady. He would make a good husband. But not for her.

Through Calum she had discovered that she was capable of a much deeper emotion than Steve had ever aroused. It meant that marriage to Steve would be second best. She would always hanker after something more, something he could not give.

'I—I've got a job here,' she managed, and sensing the shock at the other end of the line went on quickly, 'working for Mr McEwen. In that way, Steve, I shall be able to meet more people and ask more questions, and hopefully discover the truth about the cottage more quickly. He's going to pay me twice what I got off old Spindleton, so don't you see, it's too good an opportunity to miss.' She was talking too quickly and she knew it, but she did not want to give Steve an opportunity to voice his disapproval.

After she had finished there was a pause which told her more than words what he thought of the idea. When he spoke his voice was thick. 'What's this McEwen like?'

'Oh, you needn't worry,' she cried, 'he's perfectly hateful. I can't stand him really, and it will give me the greatest pleasure to tell him that the cottage is mine after all. He locked me out, would you believe? But I broke a window and got in that way. We've had quite a few words, but——'

'Holly!' Steve sounded distraught. 'I don't like it. You can't stay there. If you get on the wrong side of him in that God forsaken hole who's to say what he will do?'

'It's sorted out,' she said. 'We understand each other now. He won't hurt me.'

'I'm not so sure. Oh, Holly, please come home.' The anguish in his voice brought a lump to Holly's throat. 'I wish I'd never let you go. Forget the damn cottage, it's not worth it.'

'To me it is,' she returned steadily. 'It's a matter of justice. Calum McEwen's so filthy rich that it can't mean anything to him, but it means a lot to me. I'm fighting it through, Steve, and you can't stop me.'

'How old is this McEwen?' asked Steve next, a different note entering his voice. Suspicion now, wondering whether her vehement refusal covered something she was trying to hide.

'Quite old,' she said, because to her he was.

'Is he married?'

'No, and he has no intention of ever getting married, so if you're thinking the attraction lies in him, forget it. I'm after my pound of flesh, that's all. I've no interest in him as a man.' Who was she trying to kid? But that was the way it had to be, so she might as well get used to the idea.

'And do you still love me?'

She smiled sadly into the receiver. 'Yes, Steve, I love you.' Because in her own way she did. She had not simply fallen out of love with him because she had met Calum. She had discovered it wasn't the right kind of love to base a marriage on, but she was still very fond of him all the same.

'You will be careful?'

'I'll be careful,' she promised. 'Will you tell my parents? I'll write to them soon. Now I must go. I'm using McEwen's phone.'

'From what you say he can afford it,' said Steve gruffly. 'Take care of yourself, my love. I hope you know what you're doing. Keep in touch.'

'I will,' she said, 'and, thank you, for . . . understanding.' Then she put down the phone before he could say he did not understand, nor would he, not in a thousand years.

She turned to find Calum McEwen standing in front of the fireplace, a glass of whisky in his hand, an inscrutable expression on his face.

'How long have you been there?' she demanded, casting her mind back over what she had said. 'How much have you heard?'

'Enough to hear what you think of me,' came the cool response. 'Was lover-boy convinced?'

'About what?' she snapped.

'Your hatred for me? I rather gained the impression that he was jealous.'

'He got the picture,' she said tightly.

'Did he object to you working for me?'

'What do you think?' Holly looked at him coldly.

'But you convinced him that you were doing the right thing? I can't say I think much of him as a man. I would have certainly wanted to know much more about the situation. In fact I'd probably have ordered you right back, or at least come up and had a look for myself what was going on.'

Incensed by his condescending attitude Holly shot across the room, coming to a halt immediately in front of him, tilting her chin belligerently. 'Steve knows I am capable of looking after myself.'

'But Steve does not know me.' There was a wicked smile on his face. 'Nor did you tell him that you would be sleeping here. Was it a deliberate omission—or did it simply slip your mind?'

Holly coloured uncomfortably. 'I saw no reason why he should know. He's worried enough. He didn't accept it as meekly as you seem to think.'

'But he did accept it,' said Calum, 'which tells me what type of man he is.'

And I know what type you are, she thought. Too

damned sexy for my peace of mind. Even when they argued, which seemed to be all the time, there was no denying his physical attraction. She knew it was going to be very difficult during the next few days to keep her feelings hidden.

There was a primitive earthiness about him that simply could not be ignored. It was no wonder he had had to get rid of his other secretaries. It would be impossible to work for him without reacting most strongly to his undeniable male magnetism. Any women who could ignore the erotic vibes that emanated from him would need to be made of stone.

Even that afternoon when he had taken her to the office in the west wing of the house she had listened more to the erratic beat of her heart than to what he was saying.

'Are you quite sure you understand?' His tone had been terse following a lengthy explanation after which she had looked at him blankly, not having heard one word he had said.

'If you wouldn't mind going through it again?' Her wide eyes had rested on the rugged handsomeness of his face, and a muscle had jerked angrily in his jaw as he repeated his instructions.

'I hope I've not made a mistake,' he said coldly. 'A secretary I need, a half-wit I can do without.'

But when he had gone she managed to get through quite a lot of the work, which proved self-explanatory when she looked at it properly, when he was not there to take her mind off such mundane matters as sorting enquiries from invoices, letters which needed urgent replies from those which could wait a few days.

She had not known he owned a whisky distillery. This had been a complete surprise. 'We make whisky in a very small way at the moment,' he told her, 'and all the paper work is dealt with here as you can see. But I intend to expand and this office will then be moved.'

She was impressed. 'My grandfather called whisky the Water of Life. He never missed his night-time tot.'

'It was given that name before it was called whisky,' informed Calum. '*Uisge beatha*, in Gaelic. A by-product of your typical Scottish thrift that you're so fanatic about. Rather than waste their surplus barley farmers used to mash and ferment it, then distil it. And, of course, the secret of good Scotch whisky is Scotch water.'

Holly laughed. 'What difference does that make? I think you're kidding me.'

'I'm perfectly serious,' he said. 'If you look you'll often find that distilleries are situated in glens or near tumbling streams.'

'And is yours near here?' asked Holly.

'Naturally,' came the immediate reply. 'What better use could be put to the soft water that is our natural heritage? You cannot see the distillery from the cottage, it is higher up the glen where it does not detract from the view. It's siting was given much thought.'

'I'm glad to hear it,' she said primly. 'I might take a walk up there one day and have a look. I'd like to see how whisky is made. Would anyone mind?'

He grinned unexpectedly. 'I'll take you myself. It will be a pleasure. You're the first secretary who's shown any interest. All they usually want is a pay packet at the end of the week. You really are a remarkable woman, young Holly.'

She glowed warmly at this praise, and determined to

do the job to the best of her ability, concentrating so fiercely that when he sought her out again she was surprised how late it was.

'I've fetched your things from the cottage,' he said. 'Perhaps you'd like to wash and change before dinner? You travel remarkably light for a woman. My congratulations.'

She wondered whether he was mocking her, whether he had guessed she intended staying overnight only. 'I didn't think I'd need much,' she improvised. 'I never dreamed I'd be staying anywhere so grand. I hope you'll forgive me if I appear underdressed.' She had the strangest feeling that he might dress up for dinner. Some people did that, she knew, even if they lived alone.

'I promise not to show you up,' he laughed. And he hadn't. Looking at him now as they stood face to face in front of the blazing log fire she realised he had kept to his word. Gone was his riding habit, replaced with a pair of brown corduroy trousers that moulded every inch of his muscular thighs, and a green checked, discreetly casual shirt, unbuttoned halfway to reveal a smooth tanned chest that beckoned to her fingers each time she looked at it.

Ironically he wore similar gear to that she was used to seeing Steve in, yet on this man they looked different. On Steve they were nondescript, on Calum they looked—superb. They fitted him in the manner that only expensive clothes could and he looked so essentially masculine and virile and irresistible that it was difficult to remain angry.

'Are you ready for dinner?' he asked blandly. 'We'll have Hamilton champing at the bit if we keep him waiting much longer.'

The meal was, as she had expected, excellent, and Calum unusually charming. All in all it was a very pleasant evening and when she eventually went up to her room she felt none of the antagonism she had experienced at their first meeting.

In fact, when the door closed behind her she felt a teeny bit disappointed. He had remained the perfect host, saying not one word out of place, behaving with the utmost respectability and politeness. It was not what she expected of him.

The bed was comfortable, even though the room was austere and she slept deeply, not waking until eight, then hurrying down to breakfast afraid she might have kept Calum waiting.

Hamilton informed her that the laird had already breakfasted. 'He's making sure all is ready for the new herd of cows,' he said. 'I doubt you'll see much of him today, Miss Burns.'

He gave her no time for further conversation, leaving the room silently on his softly slippered feet. He unnerved her, this dour man with the piercing eyes and pallid grey skin. And he did not like her, she could tell, yet she could not imagine why. Perhaps he thought that she, too, had designs on his master? It could be that the thought of a woman taking over in his house was abhorrent to him. He need have no fear. Calum did not see her in that light at all.

She shrugged mentally before lifting lids off the silver dishes on the sideboard, discovering bacon and mushrooms, sausages, tomatoes and eggs. Although a slice of toast or bowl of porridge would have done equally as well she piled her plate and surprisingly ate it all.

'It's the change of air,' she told herself after she had

finished her second cup of tea and made her way through the maze of corridors to the office.

She discovered written instructions in an untidy black hand, signed with a bold C. Time fled and when a plump elderly woman brought her a cup of tea and a couple of oatcakes she was surprised to discover it was after eleven.

'I'm the housekeeper,' said the woman. 'Maggie Duncan.' She folded her arms over her ample bosom and looked as though she was prepared to stay and talk. 'Let's hope you last a bit longer than the others. The poor man has no luck at all.'

Holly smiled. 'I hope I do as well. It's a lovely place to work. I think I'm really lucky to have got the job.'

'You're early, though,' said Maggie. 'We weren't expecting you until next week.'

'Oh, I'm not Miss Drummond,' said Holly at once. 'I'm replacing her. My name's Holly Burns. My grandparents used to live at Braeside. Did you know them?' Here was her first opportunity to ask questions and she had no intention of wasting it.

But immediately all signs of friendliness left the woman's face. 'Aye, I knew them. A pity you weren't around when you were needed.'

Before Holly could ask what she meant the woman shuffled out and closed the door none too gently behind her. Holly got up, intending to follow and ask what was meant by this unexpected reprimand, but then she thought better of it and sank back into her chair.

But it was disturbing all the same. It was not pleasant to know you were being put in the wrong without being told what you had done. Why had her grandparents needed her? Wouldn't they have got in touch if they had? There were always cards and letters at Christmas and on her birthday, there had never been any hint that they were in any sort of trouble.

She knew she should have come to see them, but that had been her mother's fault rather than hers. She was the one who had put her foot down; and lately, well, there had been Steve. Steve never wanted to visit Scotland. 'It always rains,' he had said. 'And there's nothing to do. No thanks, it's not for me.' And because she had loved him, or because she had thought she loved him, she had spent her weekends and holidays with him, promising herself that one day she would go to see them. That one day had never come—and now it was too late.

But that did not mean it was her fault they had died. It had been a tragic incident, admittedly, and she was shocked and horrified by it, but it was not one that could have been averted. No one could have done anything about it.

The housekeeper's remarks, however, stayed with Holly for the rest of the morning and she found it difficult to concentrate. Calum put in an appearance at lunchtime and she told him what Maggie had said. He smiled kindly and put his big warm hand over hers. 'I shouldn't worry about Maggie. She talks too much, but she's an excellent housekeeper and I wouldn't be without her.'

'I can't think what she meant, though,' insisted Holly. 'She's made me feel as though it was my fault they died.'

He smiled and gently pulled her against him. 'No one knows quite how Maggie's mind works. Don't let it worry you. There was nothing you could have done.'

She allowed him to hold her, feeling soothed by the hard hand that brushed her hair back from her brow, feeling some of the tension drain from her. He smelled of fresh air and fragrant peat and she had a sudden longing to be out there on the windswept hillsides with him.

'I don't think I could concentrate on work this afternoon,' she said, smiling shyly up at him. 'Would you mind if I came out with you?'

He looked surprised, but nodded at once, the pressure of his arms increasing. 'It will be pleasure, Holly, so long as it doesn't become a habit. Not that I don't enjoy your company, I do, but——'

'It's not what you're paying me for,' she finished pertly.

He flicked her cheek with his finger. 'Careful what you're saying, you young minx. I had to punish you once, remember? I might just well do it again.'

How could she have forgotten a kiss that had drained every ounce of resistance from her? A kiss that had awoken her senses and made her aware of herself as a woman. A kiss that had told her she did not love Steve enough to marry him!

Quite unconsciously she ran her tongue over her lips, aware that her heart was beating faster than normal and that he must surely feel it against him. She put her hands on the solid wall of his chest and tried to push away, but his grip tightened.

'Where are you going? You've gone rigid again. Is the thought of me kissing you so unpalatable?'

She could not look at him for fear he might read the truth on her face, but when he fixed a firm finger beneath her chin, tilting her head inexorably upwards, there was no escape.

A shiver ran through her as she looked into the darkness of his half-hooded eyes. Her limbs grew weak and she knew that she wanted this kiss more than anything in the world. But even so she shook her head. 'No, Calum, no,' she husked. 'Please don't.'

'Why, when you want it as much as me? Why deny your body the pleasure it craves?' His voice was deep and sensual and very persuasive.

Somewhere beneath her shoulder Holly felt his heart beats quicken and was stimulated by the knowledge that he, too, found the thought of kissing her exciting. 'Because it—it's not right,' she managed to whisper.

'Because of Steve?' he growled. 'That passive little man you profess to love? Who's to say he's not enjoying himself in your absence? You don't belong to him yet, Holly, why not enjoy yourself while you can?'

'Steve's not passive,' she demurred, but knew she was weakening. Calum's hands moved with treacherous expertise over her back, sliding beneath the soft wool of her sweater. His fingertips seared her naked skin, becoming more and more persuasive as he moulded her against the muscled hardness of his body.

Holly knew that she could not hold out much longer and when his mouth finally came down on hers she felt herself drowning in a whirlpool of ecstasy. Of their own volition her hands crept round his neck, her fingers mingling in the crisp wavy hair that had tempted her from the beginning.

She moulded the shape of his head, holding him close as his kisses became more intense, and this time there was no resisting. Flames of delight shot through her as his kiss deepened, his tongue tasting and probing, exploring the intimate softness of her mouth.

It had never been like this with Steve. His kisses were mild and pleasant but did not evoke these unbelievable sensations that caused her head to spin and her legs to weaken. She would never have suspected that such feelings were possible.

She arched even closer towards Calum, pressing her slim shaking body against his, aware of his arousal, feeling wave after wave of sheer unadulterated desire course through her.

When Calum put her from him she could not accept that he wanted to end this exalted arousal that was like nothing she had ever experienced, and she clutched him, her beautiful luminous eyes questioning, imploring.

He shook his head briefly. 'I don't want to stop, my beautiful Holly, but it is best. I never thought you would—respond like that. Steve's a lucky guy.' His voice was gruff and he looked annoyed with himself, muscles jerking unevenly in his jaw.

'Of course you knew,' snapped Holly, angry because he knew how to handle himself whereas she was still highly excited. 'Just the same as you know what you're doing now. It's no wonder your secretaries leave, if this is how you treat them. They must be as frustrated as hell.'

'Holly.' He put his hands on her shoulders and because she had not the strength to fight she stood meekly. 'It's not like that at all. You're different, that's why I can't—take advantage.'

'So you admit you did take advantage of the others?' she flung crossly, longing more than anything to feel him against her again. The ache in her stomach was indescribable. It was sheer torture standing there, every nerve screaming for fulfilment, knowing that he did not find her as irresistible as she did him.

Miraculously he pulled her against him, enfolding her gently in his long powerful arms. 'They did the chasing,' he said sadly. 'They deserved what they got. Believe me, I never gave any one of them any encouragement.'

'Then why did you kiss me?' Her voice was muffled against his chest, and she felt close to tears.

'Because you're different, little Holly. I wanted to see whether you were tough right the way through or whether beneath that fiery façade there is a warm passionate woman.'

'And now you know.' She was glad he could not see her face. She began to feel ashamed for responding the way she had, especially as it had been nothing more than an experiment so far as he was concerned.

'You feel you've let your boyfriend down? It's not so, Holly. Some women are capable of loving one man and feeling a physical attraction for another. Men, too, for that matter. But it will not happen again unless you want it to, I promise you that.'

Was that all she felt for Calum—physical attraction? Once she left here would she forget this big man with the sexy body? She wished she could accept that, but unfortunately Calum had now spoilt her for Steve. Things would never be the same between them again.

'I think it's time we went for that walk.' He sounded as reluctant as she to move.

'I've changed my mind,' she said, keeping her face well hidden in his shirt. Lord, she wanted to go with him, but it was far too dangerous a thing to do. He was not good for her peace of mind. The reason she had come to this house was to establish the truth about the cottage, not indulge in an affair. Because surely that was what would happen? She would be unable to resist him and Calum, for all his fine words, was a virile man. He would not be able to keep his hands off her for long.

'You're not allowed to.' There was laughter in his voice now, all emotion had faded. 'You could do with a dose of fresh air.'

'Are those orders?' She attempted to match his levity, but it was difficult when she felt twisted and torn inside, as though he had taken her heart and crushed it in his big hands, heedless of the pain he was causing.

He surprised her by swinging her up into his arms. 'Very much so, Miss Holly Burns. Are you daring to defy me?'

She could not read the expression in his eyes. Nor had she any wish to. It was too disturbing by far looking into that carved handsome face, feeling the heat of desire rage through her limbs. 'I don't think I'd stand a chance.'

'At last you're being sensible.' He put her down and tucked her arm though his. 'I'll show you my new Ayrshires. They're a fine sight and no mistake.'

Hamilton came in to collect their dishes and Holly, in her heightened state, felt his disapproval even more strongly than before. It was clear to her now that he felt the same way as Maggie, except that he had no intention of putting his thoughts into words. He contented himself with speaking glances.

She shivered and clung to Calum. It seemed that he was her only friend in this great big house. If she could call him that. He had been far from friendly to begin with and it was probably only because he was getting his own way that he was nice to her now.

If he had listened to all of her conversation with

Steve he would know she was here for one reason only. Except that somehow the importance of proving that she was the rightful owner of Braeside was fading. She no longer wanted to fight Calum. As quickly as that she had changed her mind, like she had changed her mind about Steve. She felt very mixed up.

CHAPTER FIVE

THE next few days passed uneventfully. Calum was companionable and friendly but nothing more and they began to build up a good relationship.

Maggie and Hamilton between them ran the house on well-oiled wheels and Holly saw little of them. When they did meet they made no attempt to hide their disapproval and dislike. One thing was clear, she would never get any information from them.

On Friday the electricity was turned back on at the cottage, but Calum suggested it would be easier, while she was working for him, if she stayed at the house. 'Of course,' he said, 'if you insist, I cannot keep you here. But I do think it would be best. I sometimes need letters typing urgently. I should hate you to have to make that two mile journey for the sake of one letter.'

Although Holly did not entirely believe that his excuse was altruistic she agreed, partly because of her growing attraction towards him, partly because she did not want to be alone in the cottage.

She had told Calum that the way her grandparents died did not bother her but now she found that it did. She laid the blame on Maggie and Hamilton. It was their attitude that was making her feel uncomfortable. She almost wished she had never come here, except that Calum more than compensated for her distress.

She tried to phone Steve on several occasions but always he was out. It made her wonder whether

Calum had been right and he was taking advantage of her absence. Mandy Tranter would be willing to see him at any time.

Mandy had been his girlfriend when Holly met him, and although Holly had tried to tell her that she had not deliberately set out to attract Steve, Mandy refused to listen and there had been open enmity between them since. Now Mandy would be having a field day, Holly was sure.

It was a surprise, therefore, when Steve turned up on Saturday evening. She and Calum were listening to records in a small cosy room he called his den. He had a weakness for bagpipes and was trying to convince Holly that there was no other sound to beat them. They were involved in a laughing debate when Maggie tapped on the door and pushed it open.

'A visitor for Miss Burns,' she said, looking at Holly as though she had no right to receive anyone in this house. 'A Mr Kelly.'

Holly had already caught sight of Steve standing a few paces behind the roly-poly woman and sprang to her feet, her laughter now a warm smile of welcome. 'Steve! This is a surprise. Why didn't you let me know you were coming?'

'Seems I should have done,' he said, pecking her cheek before turning to Calum. 'Mr McEwen, I presume? I'm sorry to intrude but I expected to find Holly at the cottage.' There was cold censure in his voice. 'It was quite a shock to discover it empty. I've spent hours searching for her.'

'I'm sorry,' said Calum, standing up and holding out his hand. 'We had no idea you were on your way.'

Steve took it hesitantly and Holly could not help comparing the two men. Calum was a head taller than

Steve, making him look puny in comparison, and it was to Calum her eyes were drawn.

He was assessing the younger man shrewdly, although Steve did not know it, and she wondered what thoughts were going through his mind. He had never hidden his contempt of the man who had let his girlfriend travel to the wilds of Scotland alone, and then calmly accepted that she was staying on because there was a dispute over the cottage.

But none of this showed on his face. He gave a welcoming smile, although Holly knew Calum well enough by now to realise that it was not completely genuine. 'You must be hungry after your journey. I'll ask Hamilton to fix some supper. If you'd like to freshen up Holly will show you the way.'

As soon as the door closed Steve turned on Holly, but instead of the loving embrace she anticipated he said crossly, 'I must say you've made yourself very much at home. I thought you hated the man?' A frown creased his normally smooth brow and there were lines of strain about his mouth that could have been due to the journey, but were probably dissatisfaction because Holly was not where he had expected.

'I'm sorry you had trouble finding me,' she said moving forward and sliding her hands round his waist, realising she did not have to tilt back her head to look into his face as she did with Calum. 'I wish you'd written. I've phoned every night but you've been out. Oh, Steve, it is good to see you.'

'I can't think you mean that,' he grumbled, putting her from him impatiently, shoving his hands deep into his trouser pockets and eyeing her resentfully. 'You appear to be having a good time. How often does this happen?'

'Does what happen?' This was a side of Steve she had never seen before. Always they had enjoyed a harmonious relationship. The only time they had ever argued was over her coming up here.

'You know what I mean,' he gruffed. 'This socialising—with *him.*' He spat out the word as though it left a nasty taste in his mouth.

'I do work for Calum,' said Holly quietly. 'You surely don't think that there's anything going on between us?' Was that what it had looked like?

Steve shook his head in bewilderment. 'I don't know what to think. It's obviously not the first time you've been together like this. You were too relaxed. Do you spend all your evenings here?'

It occurred to her that he thought she was living at the cottage, and too late she wished she had told him over the phone. He was not going to take to the idea very kindly. 'As a matter of fact,' she said hesitantly, 'I'm living here at the moment. There was no electricity on at the cottage and it seemed a good idea when Calum suggested it, so I——'

'My God,' said Steve, a fanatical light appearing in his eyes which made Holly feel suddenly afraid. 'I was out of my mind with worry when you weren't at the cottage, but I never dreamt that you were sleeping with that man. You cheap little——'

'I'm not, I'm not,' she cried, holding up her hands to ward him off as he pounced on her. 'Steve, believe me, there's nothing in it. We've become—friends, but that is all.'

It was an effort to hold his gaze, but somehow she managed it, watching his emotions pass from blazing jealousy to doubt and finally to reluctant acceptance. 'I'm sorry, Holly, it's just that I'm so tired.'

He ran his fingers through his hair. 'It's been a hell of a day. And then to find you here like this. I know I shouldn't have doubted you, you're the straightest girl I've ever known, but I couldn't help myself. I——' He groaned and pulled her into his arms.

'It's all right, Steve,' she said against his chest. 'It was natural you should think that. But there's nothing between us, I assure you.' There was no smell here of sweet-scented heather, or horses, or even cows. Nothing but stale tobacco.

Had she been in Calum's arms now she would have felt an upsurge of emotion, a clamouring of the senses. Instead there was nothing, and she was surprised that her feelings could change so quickly. Only a week ago there had been no doubt in her mind that this was the man she would one day marry. It had never occurred to her that she would meet a man who would change her entire outlook practically overnight.

It was difficult to fix a genuine smile to her lips, a smile that needed to convince Steve that nothing was wrong. But she must have succeeded for he squeezed her tightly and said, 'I believe you, Holly. But I don't want you to stay here. I want you to come home with me.'

A stab of dismay shot through her at the thought of leaving Calum, and in the light of her burgeoning feelings for this big man the ownership of the cottage lost its importance. But all the same she said weakly to Steve, 'I—I can't, I haven't found out about the cottage.'

'Nor will you,' he snapped. 'He'll see to that. Let your solicitor deal with it. I don't want you here, it's as simple as that. I don't care how much he's paying you, it's just not on. There's nothing in it now, but if you stay much longer there will be. I can see it happening.' He let her go and began pacing up and down.

'No, Steve,' said Holly, 'Calum's a confirmed bachelor, he made a point of telling me that.'

'And you told me you were fighting for your rights. But the way you were when I came into the room, I can't see it. He's using you, Holly, he's taking advantage of your sentimentality over the cottage to keep you here. I imagine he has difficulty in getting anyone to work for him in this God forsaken place.'

'Steve, Glen Shilda is beautiful,' she protested immediately. 'How can you say that? I'd forgotten quite how enchanting it is. It's not changed one little bit. I'd like to live here.'

Not until she had made this rash statement did Holly realise it was true. It surprised her as much as it did Steve.

'You don't mean that?' His pale blue eyes widened. 'You're not asking that I give up my job and——' His voice tailed. 'No, that's not what you mean at all. You've fallen for McEwen, that's it, isn't it? You're hoping it will only be a matter of time before he feels the same about you. I never thought of you as a temptress, Holly, I'm disappointed. It looks as though I've come not a minute too soon. Get your things. I've booked in at an hotel in Invercray. You can come with me.'

If she did it would mean she would never see Calum again. It would be for the best, undoubtedly, since there could be nothing between them but friendship. He had made that plain. After that last experimental kiss he had made no further advances. He had tested a theory and was satisfied. From now on she was his secretary and companion and nothing more. If she showed signs of getting amorous she would be turned out as had all the others.

It was not a very satisfying relationship, and in her own interests she knew she ought to go with Steve, yet the attraction here was so much stronger. She found herself shaking her head without consciously knowing that she was doing it. 'I can't let him down, Steve.'

He shot her a contemptuous glance. 'If you hated him as much as you professed after that first meeting you wouldn't give a damn. What the hell's got into you, Holly? You've changed. You're not the same girl.'

She smiled weakly. 'Perhaps it's my Scottish ancestry. I just know I want to stay here—it's a feeling I have. This is where I belong, Steve.'

'With McEwen?' he asked bitterly.

'No!' Holly shook her head quickly. 'Not with Calum. At Braeside. My grandparents wanted me to have it, Steve. I'm going to fight for it and I'm going to live there.'

He lifted his pale brows sceptically. 'Alone? I'm not a fool, Holly, don't take me for one. It's McEwen you're after. You can wrap it in whatever package you like, but it all boils down to the same thing.'

She was saved the need to answer when Calum came into the room. He glanced from one to the other, taking in their tense bodies and hostile eyes, but there was nothing in his voice to suggest he was aware of any undercurrents. 'Supper won't be long. You'll stay the night, of course, Steve? I've instructed Maggie to get one of the guest rooms ready.'

'Then you've wasted your time,' said Steve tightly. 'I'm leaving—now. Are you coming, Holly?'

It was an ultimatum and she hesitated, looking from the young sandy-haired man to her employer. Calum's face gave nothing away. Whatever decision she made she did it on her own—and really she would be a fool to stay. All it would do was pave the way to future heartache. If, at thirty-six, Calum had never married, there was little likelihood that he would change his mind now. She ought to go—before it was too late.

But she loved him! Not until this moment had she known her feelings ran so deep. It was a shock, and she shook her head as if trying to clear it of these futile thoughts.

Mistaking her action Steve said coldly, 'I take it that means no?'

She tore her eyes away from Calum's granite-hard face and looked at the man who had once meant so much to her. Surely it was not possible to transfer your emotions so quickly and completely? It was infatuation she felt for Calum, nothing more. He was different, he was a challenge, but it wouldn't last.

Willing herself to respond to Steve she took a step towards him, but apart from feeling compassion there was nothing else. Silently she pleaded with him to understand, unable to voice that final no.

A sigh was wrenched from deep inside him and he turned and walked out of the room, his back rigid, his actions mechanical. Holly felt awful yet what was the point in calling him back, of going with him, when there could be no future for them together? It would give him hope when there was none.

Maybe she wouldn't stay here, not for ever, there would no point in that either. But she could always hope, and she was doing Calum a good turn as well as enjoying the work.

Calum cast Holly a speculative glance and then followed Steve. She sank down on to the armchair where she had been so comfortable a few minutes earlier and dropped her head into her hands.

Who would have believed things would turn out like this? It was a mistake, remaining here, when she had an excellent excuse for leaving, but what person in love behaved rationally?

It seemed likely that she had never loved Steve. He had been a friend, that was all. There was no romance in him, he did not believe in sentimentality. The way he had casually mentioned marriage was indicative of this, So far as he was concerned it had been a foregone conclusion, there had been no need for him to flatter her with soft music and roses and a few tenderly spoken words. But she wanted more out of life than that. She wanted Calum. This was the basic truth whether she liked it or not.

With an effort she pulled herself together. She had no wish for him to see her like this. When he came into the room a few minutes later her smile was as near normal as she could manage.

He carried two suitcases which he dumped in front of her. 'Steve brought some of your clothes.'

'How thoughtful,' she said impulsively.

'Very,' came the dry reply. 'I gather he wasn't too pleased when he found you'd moved in here?'

She shook her head. 'He—he thought that we——'

'Were having an affair?' he finished for her.

Holly's cheeks coloured and she nodded.

His thick brows rose mockingly. 'Why the embarrassment? I'm quite certain you put him right on that score.'

'Of course I did,' she answered quickly. 'But——'

'He didn't believe you? You obviously weren't convincing enough. Why is that, I wonder? And why, little Holly, did you decide to stay here instead of leaving with your boyfriend when it was clearly what he wanted?'

Holly's mouth felt dry and she lowered her lids over her green eyes, unable to look at him. She felt uncomfortable and shifted uneasily in her seat. 'You know the answer,' she said softly.

'Do I?' he asked, and he sounded as though he was smiling.

She swallowed convulsively, knowing she had to be careful what she said. Calum was too perceptive by far. It would do her no good at all to reveal her feelings. In fact it would lose her her job.

With an effort she lifted her lashes. 'It's because I'm determined to prove my right to the cottage—you know that.' She was surprised to hear how clear and steady her voice sounded.

'And that is your only reason?'

For an instant she thought she saw a flicker of disappointment cross his rugged face, but it was gone so quickly she decided she was mistaken. What other answer could he have expected? 'I like working for you as well,' she admitted. 'It's interesting.'

The dark eyes never left her face. 'Go on—is there anything more?'

Because I love you, she wanted to say, but could imagine his reaction to such a dramatic announcement. His brow would darken, those infinitely kissable lips would narrow until they were invisible, and his beautiful eyes would resemble chips of black ice. He would lift an arm and with pointed finger would order her out of this house for ever. Love was an emotion he would never let into his life.

She wondered why. She could understand his objecting to girls fawning over him, but why be so resolute about not wanting to get married?

'It's taking you a long time to think about it,' he prodded impatiently.

She lifted her thin shoulders. 'There's no other reason.'

Almost as though she had admitted her love his face tightened in exactly the same manner as she had known it would. He turned away and there was an unusual gruffness to his voice when he next spoke. 'I suppose we'd better go in to supper. Hamilton will not be pleased if we, as well as Steve, don't turn up.'

Holly had never felt less like eating but she followed Calum into the room where she usually ate breakfast. There was a tureen of vegetable soup, a selection of cold meats and cheeses, pickles and crusty rolls, a rich fruit cake and mouth-watering pastries, all got ready at short notice for their unexpected visitor.

She took a roll and a curl of butter, and a tiny portion of cheese, nibbling at it delicately as Calum ate his way through a surprising amount of food. Despite all he consumed he never put on an ounce of surplus weight—unlike herself. She was sure she had already added a couple of pounds in the week she had been here.

When he finally pushed away his plate the taut lines had disappeared from his face. He was again the impersonally friendly man who had taken her into his house.

'So Steve's going home without you? I must admit when he turned up here I thought I'd misjudged him. I was ready to take back my words.'

Despite how she felt about Calum Holly was not

prepared to let him put Steve down. 'You can't blame Steve,' she said. 'He was most determined to take me back with him. He didn't like the idea of me being here; no more than you would under similar circumstances.'

He smiled humourlessly. 'I certainly wouldn't, and I'd have been a damn sight more positive than your young man. You wouldn't run rings round me, I can tell you.'

His confidence irritated Holly. 'Not even you would make me do something I didn't want to,' she said strongly. 'Why shouldn't women have minds of their own? It's a free country. I happen to like living here. I don't want to go back to the Midlands. There's no comparison.'

He looked at her speculatively, elbows on the table, fingertips touching. 'By here, you mean this house?'

'I mean Glen Shilda,' she said firmly. 'This part of Scotland. I think I may very well settle down in the cottage once it's all sorted out.'

His brows rose in that sceptical manner she was beginning to know. 'I can't imagine you being happy there for long. It's too lonely, too basic. What the hell would you do with yourself?'

'My grandparents would never have lived anywhere else. Why should it be different for me?'

There was a slight tightening to the corners of his mouth. 'They were born here, that is the difference. All you did was spend holidays here, and for the last— ten years is it? you've been nowhere near the place. No, Holly, I don't think you'd be happy.'

With you, I would, her heart cried. But she ignored that and said thickly, 'It just shows how little you know me.'

'I know that modern misses brought up in busy towns don't take easily to this kind of life. Do you propose dragging Steve up here too? I reckon he'll take a bit of persuading. Do you think you can manage it?' There was a glint of humour in his eyes as he looked at her across the table.

Steve would never live here, she knew that, but she had no intention of telling Calum this. Steve was the buffer she needed to protect herself. 'He'll get used to the idea,' she said, her chin jutting determinedly, her green eyes flashing in the soft light from the converted oil-lamp.

'Your grandfather worked for the McEwens,' he said, 'before he retired. But we're fully manned now. Where do you reckon he'll find work? What is he trained for?'

'He's a welder,' admitted Holly reluctantly, 'but there's no reason why he shouldn't do something else.'

'Sheep shearing?' mocked Calum, 'or fishing, perhaps? Or he might even set himself up in one of the cottage industries that abound in this area. Could you see him knitting an arran sweater, or weaving a length of tweed?'

'You're hateful,' snapped Holly.

'I'm merely being practical,' he said. 'It's about time you took your head out of the clouds, my little spitfire. Living here would not work at all.'

'Because you don't want me to, I suppose.' Holly crumbled her half-eaten roll between her fingers without even knowing she was doing it, arranging the pieces in a circle round the edge of her plate.

'Let's say you'd be a very disruptive influence.' Before she could ask what he meant he scraped his chair back from the table. 'I'll take your cases to your room. I expect you'd like to unpack, unless you wish to go to the cottage now?' There was a bleakness in his eyes, a sudden unexpected change of mood.

'Is that what you want me to do?'

He looked at her for a long moment. 'It would be best but not convenient. You may as well stay.'

When he had gone Holly wondered what had wrought this change. She'd be disruptive, he had said, and before that she had questioned him wanting her here. Was that it? Had he imagined she was angling for sympathy? If only he knew!

Holly remained in her seat until she was quite sure she would not meet him in her room, then made her way upstairs. She glanced angrily at the portraits of McEwens past, wondering if they had all been as unpredictable as this man. She never knew where she was with him. He could be friendly one moment hostile the next, he could be the impersonal employer explaining what he wanted doing, or as tender and teasing as a lover. He was as changeable as the wind.

In her room she flicked open the cases, smiling wryly at Steve's attempts at packing. Her clothes were rolled rather than folded, crammed into corners, shoes next to delicate underwear, no thought given at all to the condition they would be in when they were unpacked.

She hung dresses and blouses on hangers in the vain hope that the creases would fall out, folded jumpers and lingerie into drawers, and placed her shoes in a neat row in the bottom of the wardrobe.

After that she glanced at her watch. It was almost ten but she knew that if she went to bed she would not sleep. It was a clear night with an almost full moon. A walk down to the waters of the loch would do her the world of good.

She pulled on a blue cardigan that had surprisingly survived its crushing treatment and quietly let herself out of the house. Since coming to work here she had been no further than the grounds themselves. They were beautiful with their tall Scots firs and the spreading chestnuts, sloping lawns immaculately kept by unseen gardeners, great banks of rhododendrons and hosts of flowers all anxious to show off their perfect blooms.

But she wanted to escape all this tonight. She needed exercise, she needed to tire herself out if she was to sleep. It had been a momentous discovery, realising she loved Calum, and the fact that there was nothing at all she could do about it made it all the harder to bear.

Owls hooted in the forest, in the undergrowth tiny animals scuttled for safety. As a child she had never been allowed out once it was dark, now she discovered an entirely new world.

Each shape took on a different meaning, each sound was magnified. She stood still for a moment and was conscious that the forest came into its own at night. The wind stirred the branches of the great trees, whistling through the leaves, sending shivers down slender stems.

She took a step or two further and caught sight of a herd of deer, motionless beneath the trees, the filtered moonlight picking out their dark shapes, wary of her approach, ready to run should she get too close. Calum had told her about the roe deer, but this was the first glimpse she had caught of them.

Unwilling to frighten them by going any nearer she left the forest and made her way down the track towards the loch. It reflected the ghostly light of the moon, its rippled surface a brilliant sheet of beaten silver.

On the bridge she stopped and leaned over the wall, looking down at her reflection. Silent ducks sailed aloofly by, there was the occasional splash as a trout broke the surface, and all around were the magical scents that could be found nowhere else except in the Scottish Highlands.

Holly turned and leaned back against the moss-covered stonework, closing her eyes and inhaling the sweet freshness of unadulterated air, listening to the trickle of water from the dozens of burns that spilled down the hillside. She could be happy here, she knew. It was like coming home.

Glen Shilda was as unlike England, or at least her part of England, as it was possible for two places to be. Nowhere in Walsall could she go and be as alone as she was in this vast place. Nowhere could the silence close in around her until it felt as though it was a bubble waiting to burst.

She would never be bored here and since she had no intention now of marrying Steve she would move into her little cottage as soon as her job was finished, which she hoped would not be for a long time yet. She would be as happy as a pig in muck polishing and cleaning, redecorating and cooking.

Or would she? No girl in her right mind would shut herself off from civilisation because of unrequited love. She was being foolish. She was letting her infatuation get the better of her. The very best thing she could do was go right away from here, go back to Walsall, throw herself into her work heart and soul, and forget all about Calum.

She opened her eyes and he was standing right in front of her. Her cry of alarm was checked when his mouth closed on hers, when a pair of strong arms held her close. Without conscious thought Holly gave herself up to the ecstasy of the moment.

CHAPTER SIX

THERE was no passion in Calum's kiss, and it lasted no longer than a few seconds, yet it affected Holly to such an extent that she felt as though the world was spinning about her head. She gazed up at him, eyes wide with wonder.

'What are you doing, little girl in the night?' His lips curved mockingly and the moonlight turned his face to polished bronze. 'Deliberating whether you have made the wrong choice? Do you think that after all you should have gone with your young man?'

As that was precisely the decision she had reached Holly was astonished at the accuracy of his guess, but was also determined not to let him know that he was right. 'Of course not,' she said brightly. 'It's such a fine night I thought I'd take a walk.'

'It wasn't because you thought you might have difficulty in sleeping after your—er, disagreement with your visitor?'

'Steve and I haven't fallen out,' she said swiftly, resenting the way he kept flinging Steve at her.

'No? It wasn't the impression he gave me. He seemed to think it was the end of the road.' He leaned back on the wall at her side and Holly was more aware than ever of his aggressive masculinity. It stole over her like a cloak, warming her limbs, making her vibrantly responsive to his nearness, feeling a heady sensation that could not be calmed.

'He was upset, naturally, when he found I was

living here, but he understands how important the cottage is to me, and he knows that I shan't rest until I've discovered the truth.'

She heard the soft laughter which broke from Calum's lips, and in her heightened state its sensuousness unnerved her. She edged an inch or two away but it made no difference. They could have been at opposite ends of the bridge and she would have still felt this tingling awareness.

'You don't seem to have done much about it so far,' he said.

'Considering how hard you've worked me I've hardly had time.' Holly took refuge in anger.

'Are you complaining?' A hand reached out for her chin, tilting her head so that she was compelled to look at him. His eyes were expressionless, deep black pools set in that sculptured face.

Holly was glad it was dark so that he could not see the flush that must surely be glowing in her cheeks. It was a cool night, yet she felt as though she was on fire and it was an effort to stop herself from trembling beneath his touch.

She could feel the hard bones of his fingers pressing into her chin, was aware of the strength in his arm, the power in his body. For all her months of training in the art of self defence this was one man she would never get the better of.

'There'd be no point, would there?' she replied tightly. 'I took the job on and I'm not the sort of person to chicken out simply because there's more to it than I expected.'

'That suggests you're putting me before Steve,' said Calum smoothly. 'No wonder he looked like a man who'd been kicked while he was down.'

Holly wrenched from the hand that gripped her and walked a few steps back the way she had come. 'Don't flatter yourself,' she thrust savagely. 'Once I've proved my ownership you won't see me again. Unless of course it's by accident—and I shall do my very best to avoid that.'

'But you do intend living at Braeside—if you're successful?'

Holly nodded, not caring that she was committing herself to something that was very unwise.

'In that case there's every chance we shall meet. Glen Shilda is far too small a place to avoid your neighbours.'

'We shall see,' she flung bitterly, knowing she had no wish to avoid him. Calum made her feel more vibrantly alive than Steve ever had. He evoked a response that was primitive and basic and essentially feminine. It was sheer madness wanting to be a part of his life when she meant nothing at all to him. It could lead only to destruction. Yet what could she do about it?

Without waiting to see whether he followed she quickened her steps and was soon back at the house. Her walk had not soothed her as she hoped, due entirely to Calum's unexpected appearance, and it was a long time before she finally slept.

Normally she breakfasted alone, Calum already having eaten and gone out to look over his estate. His factor, Duncan Gillies, whom she had yet to meet, took care of everything, but even so, Calum felt that the personal involvement was still necessary.

The next morning, however, he was at the table when she went down. She had put on an apple-green dress instead of the jeans which had been her uniform since she arrived, the man-made fibre resisting Steve's ruthless packing better than anything else. Its gently gathered skirt was entirely feminine and swung about her slender legs, and the fitted bodice emphasised the pert thrust of her breasts. She wore high heels for the first time, too, and brushed her hair until it shone, applying make-up to hide the effect of her sleepless night.

It had been for her own peace of mind that she had done this, but when she noticed the flicker of admiration in Calum's eyes she was glad.

'A transformation indeed!' he commented drily. 'Steve has his usefulness after all. I'd begun to despair of ever seeing your legs. No, don't sit down, let me look at you. It's really quite extraordinary.'

'What is?' asked Holly briskly, feeling an idiot standing there while he subjected her to an intimate and insolent appraisal. He began with her face, noting with amusement her heightened colour, the nervous brilliance in her green eyes. Then he descended slowly down her slender throat, over her pointed breasts which tingled as his eyes rested upon them, following the gentle curve of her hips before finally studying her long legs and trim ankles, her painted toenails peeping through the straps of her sandals.

He missed nothing and she felt as though he was mentally undressing her, seeing through to her slim naked body beneath, and after a few seconds she could stand it no longer. She sat down and eyed him belligerently, aware that her deepened breathing, the quick rise and fall of her breasts, told their own story.

'The difference,' he said huskily, 'is amazing. You've turned into a very beautiful, very sexy, young woman. You're no longer the tomboy who wouldn't hesitate to throw me over her shoulder if she had the chance. You look demure, and innocent, and—dare I say it, virginal?'

'I'm glad it shows,' she said acidly, 'perhaps it will help you keep your eyes off me. I'm not one of your pedigree cattle, you know. I resent being looked at as though I'm for sale.'

'I don't buy my women,' he said, a sudden flicker of annoyance crossing his face. He wore a thin sweater in an attractive heather mixture wool. He was clean-shaven and smelled fresh and completely masculine, and Holly was not as immune to him as she tried to make out.

'So far as I can see you have no women friends,' said Holly with great daring. 'I find that rather odd.'

'And I think it is none of your business,' he returned sharply. 'But it is not my intention to argue. I thought, as you've made such good progress with the work in the office, that I'd take you to the distillery today. Do you still want to see it?'

Holly felt a little ashamed of her outburst. 'Thank you, I would like that very much.' She helped herself to a small piece of smoked haddock, deliberately keeping her eyes down so that he would not see her sudden joy at the thought of a few hours spent in his company.

'In that case,' he said, 'I'll saddle the horses. It's a pity you'll have to change, but it really is by far the pleasantest way of getting there. You do ride, I presume?'

'If I've not forgotten,' said Holly. 'I haven't been on a horse since—since the last time I was here.'

'Of course,' he laughed. 'A skinny pale little thing on that temperamental Shetland the Burns used to keep. I hadn't realised that was you.'

Holly shot a horrified glance across the table 'I don't remember you.'

'You wouldn't,' he grinned. 'I kept well out of the way. As a young man I had an abhorrence for children, especially those from the towns who never knew how to behave in the country.'

'I never left gates open,' she said indignantly. 'Grandad warned me about that.'

'But you did climb trees, and you threw rotten apples at the cows when you thought no one was looking, and you swam naked in the bottomless pool on the opposite side of the loch to the cottage. I'm sure your grandparents never gave you permission for that.'

Holly coloured furiously and he chuckled. 'I thought that would stun you. You never knew I'd seen you in the nude.'

'You're disgusting,' she shot.

'But I'm not a pervert,' he smiled, 'so you needn't worry. I can't say I wouldn't get a thrill out of seeing you in the same state of undress now, though. You've grown into a very desirable young lady.'

Holly felt a shiver of excitement as his narrowed eyes looked suggestively into hers. 'Considering your self-imposed celibacy I find that hard to believe.'

'I never said I was a celibate,' he said cheerfully, 'merely that I had no plans to get married.'

'Meaning you wouldn't be averse to the odd affair? I'm sorry, Calum, but that's simply not on. I have Steve, don't forget. I could never be so fickle.' She made herself believe this was the truth.

He seemed to be having difficulty in keeping his mouth straight. 'I was not aware that I'd suggested any such liaison?'

This was not the first time he had put her in the wrong and again she felt totally humiliated. Nevertheless she jutted her chin and looked him in the eye. 'I apologise if I jumped to conclusions. Of course I know you wouldn't dream of doing anything like that. You're far too honourable.'

His laughter was loud and unexpected. 'Now you're making me sound pompous. I'm not that at all, as you well know.' He reached out and tousled her hair. 'Eat your breakfast, carrot-top, and then, much as I hate to say this, get back into those infernal jeans. I'll have the horses waiting.'

He dropped a careless kiss on her brow as he came round the table and it was as much as Holly could do not to tremble. He really was the most confusing man she had ever met.

The thought of going out with Calum completely ruined her appetite, and she left the fish, eating half a slice of toast and drinking a glass of fresh orange, before rushing back up to her room.

She felt on top of the world all of a sudden and found a pretty ribbed sweater to go with a clean pair of jeans. It emphasised her feminine curves even more than the dress had, and with a bright scarf tied at her throat she felt equally as attractive. Her jeans were tighter than the pair she had worn all the week, moulding themselves to her hips and thighs, leaving very little to the imagination.

She saw Maggie on her way out and asked whether she would lend her an iron later so that she could press the clothes Steve had brought.

'I'll do them for you,' said the woman unexpectedly. 'Not that I want to, you understand? It's not what I think you deserve, but it is what the laird would expect.'

Some of Holly's pleasure faded. 'I wish I knew why you didn't like me, Maggie. I'm quite sure that I could not have prevented my grandfather's death, tragic though the circumstances were. It was just one of those things. No one could have anticipated it.'

The housekeeper sniffed indelicately. 'There's some as think you could, some as think you couldn't. But the least you could have done was attend the funeral. The poor folk had no one of their own. It was a terrible thing.' She shook her head and shuffled away before Holly could say anything in her own defence.

Holly wanted nothing to spoil this morning in Calum's company so she resolutely pushed her disturbed thoughts to one side, giving him a wide smile when she joined him in the yard.

He studied her thoroughly, making her pulse quicken, then said, 'I trust you're going to be able to sit the horse in those?'

She smoothed her hand over her hips. 'I suppose they are rather tight. I think I've put on some weight since I've been here. But they'll stretch.'

'Or split?' he suggested with amusement. 'It could be interesting. This is Lady. Think you'll be able to handle her?'

Holly looked at the chestnut mare that stood docilely beside Calum's black stallion. 'She's very—big,' she said nervously.

'But very obedient. She'll give you no trouble. Here's a hat, I trust it fits.'

He already had on his own black riding hat, but with his grey jodhpurs and cabled heather sweater he did not look so sinister as he had dressed in black. Or was it simply that she was getting used to him?

Holly shivered with involuntary pleasure when his

fingers brushed her chin as he fastened the hat, but missed his swift interrogative frown.

He helped her mount and then made her walk a few times round the yard before pronouncing himself satisfied that she knew how to handle the mare.

In one swift fluid movement he swung himself up on to his own horse and led the way from the yard. Lady glided behind the stallion and after a few minutes, riding with the fresh Highland wind against her face and the smell of the good earth in her nostrils Holly felt as though she could ride the mare for ever.

Calum kept a sedate pace at her side for the first mile, but the stallion was used to being put through his paces and tossed his head impatiently, whinnying loudly as if to ask what this slow march was all about.

'I'll let him have his head,' said Calum. 'Then I'll come back to you. Will you be all right?'

She nodded and watched as the black horse galloped like the wind up the hill, soon lost to sight over the ridge, only the drumming of its hooves telling her they were still going. Feeling challenged by this burst of energy Holly urged Lady into a trot and finally a canter. It felt good and she laughed aloud in sheer delight. She let the horse go her own way and was delighted when it followed the same trail Calum had ridden.

At the top of the hill she reined the mare in, shading her eyes against the glare of the sun, trying to spot Calum somewhere among those rolling hills. She had never been this way before and felt immense pleasure and satisfaction in the wide sweep of heather-clad slopes dotted with granite outcrops, relieved by trees of all shapes and sizes. Pale highland cattle cropped contentedly, the odd black-faced goat raised an inquisitive face in her direction.

There were one or two cottages which she guessed must belong to the men who worked on the estate, and that bigger one was probably the factor's. Calum had said that he lived in this direction. But of Calum himself there was no sign.

Then she saw him, a tiny black spot moving towards her. Constantly he disappeared as he followed the folds of the hills, but as he got nearer Lady pricked her ears and whickered. Holly urged her forward and the chestnut broke into a gallop. Holly felt a wild exhilaration such as she had never experienced before.

They flew over the ground so quickly it was as if the horse had wings on her heels. When they came to a dyke that ran horizontally across the hillside Lady sailed over with Holly clinging desperately, her eyes tightly closed, amazed that she was still in the saddle when they began racing again on the other side.

Apart from a few branches she had placed for Dinky, the Shetland, to jump when she was about eight, it was the first real jump Holly had ever made, and she felt quite pleased with herself. It had been an extraordinary sensation as they sailed through the air.

When they came to a hedge of hawthorn she had no qualms about letting Lady jump and it was not until they were at the half-way point that she felt her saddle slide. More than once she had thought it was a bit loose but had decided it was her imagination.

Now, though, it slipped to one side as the chestnut took the jump. Her uneven weight caused the horse to lose her footing and go down in a flurry of kicking legs and a whinny of fear.

Somehow Holly managed to kick her feet clear of the stirrups before Lady struggled to her feet. She was aware of an overwheleming sense of relief that the horse was unhurt, but felt as though every ounce of breath had been squeezed from her body.

It seemed an age that she lay there unable to move. The sun was warm and the grass smelled sweet and insects buzzed in her ears; then Lady was nudging her and she knew she ought to make the effort to get up.

Thudding hooves announced Calum's arrival before she had matched actions to thoughts. The sun was blacked out and she flickered open her eyes. She had never before seen him so concerned and it was almost worth the pain that wracked her body to have him look at her like that.

'Are you hurt?' He dropped to his knees, tearing off his cap, flinging it to one side, releasing the strap on hers and easing it off with gentle hands.

'I don't know.' Holly found it difficult to talk. 'I think I'm just winded.'

'I'd better check.' He ran exploratory fingers along her limbs, ordering her to move her arms and legs, and all the time she watched him, noting his hard masculine profile that could have been carved out of teak. Sunlight glistened in the black hair curling over the neck of his jumper and despite her weakness she felt an insane urge to run her fingers through its sensuous thickness.

The lump in her throat now had nothing to do with her accident, the sensations cascading through her were caused by Calum's touch alone. She could lie here all day and let him do this to her. She closed her eyes and gave herself up to the sweet agony of feeling those hard-skinned fingers tracing every bone in her body.

He touched her ribs, pressing gently, enquiring whether it was painful, gently rolling her over and continuing his explorations on her back. Finally he pronounced himself satisfied that nothing was broken.

Holly was sorry he had finished, but when he asked if she felt strong enough to stand she shook her head. She wanted these moments of intimacy to go on for ever.

When he sat down and let her use his lap as a cushion for her head she felt delirious. She could not have stage-managed it any better had she tried. 'You were very professional. Do you know something about first aid?'

He looked down, his face serious. 'I did a crash veterinary course once. My father thought it would be useful. Vets' fees can be very high. Another canny Scot, you see.'

She ignored this last gibe, unconsciously stiffening. 'So you had no more interest in me than if I was one of your precious animals?' The words were out before she could stop them.

'That's right,' he said. 'And I'm sure that is the way you wanted it. I mean, if I'd been Steve it would be different. But you wouldn't want me to—take advantage—surely?'

Holly had been certain he had derived as much pleasure out of the operation as she herself, now she felt put in her place and her disappointment was reflected in the downward curve of her lips, the sudden dulling of her eyes, and she turned her head quickly away.

Calum took her face between his palms and made her look at him, and now there was laughter in his eyes. 'Did you really believe that? Hell, Holly, I had the devil's own job acting impartially, only the fear that I might hurt you stopped me from crushing you into my arms.' His breathing deepened, she could feel the rise and fall of his chest against her head, and as she looked into his face she saw a sudden change in his expression. 'I want you, Holly. Do you know that?'

Mutely she shook her head, but her spirits lifted and she could not be sure whether the lark trilling on high was actually birdsong or music in her head.

'I went cold with fear when I saw you fall. Whatever made you attempt that jump?'

She smiled weakly. 'It was Lady's idea, not mine.'

'I blame myself,' he groaned. 'I should have checked the girth after you'd ridden a while. As soon as I saw Lady's saddle I knew it was my fault. Oh, Holly.' He lowered his head and kissed her mouth. 'I don't think I could have lived with myself if you'd been seriously hurt. Are you sure you're all right?'

Holly could not believe that she was hearing him correctly, and guessed she must be dreaming this beautiful moment. She smiled blissfully and looked into his eyes. 'I think I'm in heaven. I've never known you say such nice things to me before.'

'You haven't almost killed yourself before.'

'Then I must do it more often,' she heard herself say. 'I like it when you care.'

He groaned and kissed her again, his lips featherlight against hers. Feeling his restraint Holly put her arms about his neck and let him taste the honeyed sweetness of her response.

Immediately his kiss deepened and she was crushed against the rough wool of his sweater, folded in arms so powerful there could be no escape. He slid down beside her until they were lying together in the long grass.

Somewhere close at hand a bee buzzed incessantly as it made its never-ending search for honey, but Holly was conscious only of a yearning ache to be possessed by this man. In the strength of her heightened emotions all awareness of discomfort had gone. Calum was giving her what she had thought could never be hers.

She returned his kisses with a passion that should have surprised her, but didn't, it seemed very natural, the only response she wanted to make. When he had finished with her mouth he gave his attention to her face, kissing her eyes, her nose, the delicate lobes of her ears, nibbling erotically until she was squirming and helpless in his hands.

When he pulled her jumper expertly above her breasts Holly made no effort to resist. There was something primitive and exciting about making love in the open, and even the coarse irritation of the grass against her naked skin could be ignored.

Her nipples hardened beneath his touch and when he took each rosy peak in turn into his mouth her exhilaration knew no bounds. Wave after wave of pure sensuality washed over her and she found herself arching her body for more of what this sexually aggressive man had to offer.

Never with Steve had she felt such a searing emotion. It was tearing through her like a physical pain, shooting across her lower back and down her leg until she could stand it no longer and cried out.

Immediately Calum stopped, a swift frown knitting his black brows. 'Holly, what is wrong? Am I hurting you?'

When he was no longer consuming her, yet the pain remained, Holly knew it was for real. She screwed up her face and fought off a wave of nausea. 'It's my hip, I think. I must have bruised it. It wasn't until I lifted myself that I felt the pain. I'm sorry.' These last words were said quietly and shyly.

'My God, don't apologise.' Calum looked angry. 'It's my fault. My own stupid damn fault. Of all the times to choose to make love to you. I want flogging. I thought of myself, not you. How selfish can a man get.' He pulled her jumper down and she noticed that his long fingers were shaking.

She covered them with her own. 'Don't, Calum. It was what we both wanted. It was my fault as much as yours.'

He groaned and would have gathered her to him again had he not stopped himself in time. 'We must get you home,' he said, lifting her carefully to her feet, steadying her as she swayed.

Dizzy as she felt, Holly was not immune to him and clung more tenaciously than was necessary.

'Can you ride?' he asked anxiously, 'or shall I carry you?'

'All that way?' smiled Holly impertinently. 'You'd never make it.'

'I see the accident hasn't robbed you of your quick tongue,' he returned sharply, 'and I wouldn't advise you to make a bet on it. It wouldn't be the first time I've carried such a weight, although I must admit a sick calf is not half so attractive or as sweet-smelling as you.'

She dimpled and said, 'Thanks for the kind offer, but I'm quite sure I can manage the horse.'

'I think I'll have you up with me,' he said, 'it will be safer.'

Not safer for her peace of mind, thought Holly a few

minutes later. She was sitting in front of him on his stallion, Calum's arms were round her waist, the reins held loosely in his hands, his hard-muscled thighs pressed firmly against hers. Behind her back was the solid wall of his chest. With each step the horse took she rubbed against him and it was easy to forget the pain in her hip, concentrating totally on the erotic feelings the contact aroused.

It was a good job, she thought, determined after a few minutes of these heady senseless thoughts to put them from her mind, that he had insisted on her wearing a hat, otherwise she could very well have hurt her head. Perhaps she had. Perhaps that was what all this was about. It was certainly unexpected, but she could not deny that Calum's attentions were welcome.

'It's a pity about the distillery,' she said. 'I was looking forward to seeing it.'

'Another day.' His voice was sensual in her ear. 'There's plenty of time. For the moment we must concentrate on getting you better. You're to go straight to bed and I'll get Maggie to call the doctor.'

Holly turned her head quickly. 'There's no need. Your examination satisfied me. It's a bruise, nothing more. I expect I'll be a bit sore for a few days, but it's nothing worth bothering the doctor about. I'm sure he has quite enough to do.'

'You're a spunky lass,' he said.

Though the praise was small Holly glowed and when he held her that little bit more tightly she rested her head against his shoulder and wanted this moment to go on for ever.

She was sorry when they finally reached Shilda House. The horses' feet clattered on the cobbled yard, Lady having followed them faithfully all the way, and upon hearing them a young groom whom Holly had spotted occasionally exercising the horses came to take the animals away.

'Check Lady over, will you?' said Calum to the boy. 'She's had a fall. I don't think there's anything wrong, but you'd best keep your eye on her for a day or two.'

'And I,' he continued, as he carried Holly into the house, 'shall keep my eye on you.'

'That sounds like a threat,' she laughed, enjoying this new rapport. There was really no need for him to carry her, she could walk quite easily, but who was she to argue with his authority? Her hands were linked round his neck and she could feel the strong beat of his heart against her side.

'It is a threat,' he growled, kicking open her bedroom door and putting her down gently on the bed. It was the first time he had been in her room and she rather liked the thought of him here.

She resisted the temptation not to let go her hands and pull him down with her. He might very well forget her bruise and take up again where he had left off.

Not that that would be a bad thing, she thought, as he moved towards the door. At that moment, her body still tingling from the contact, she wanted him very much.

'Do you want Maggie to help you undress?' he asked gently.

Holly shook her head. Not Maggie; you, Calum! That would be sweetness indeed.

CHAPTER SEVEN

CALUM made Holly stay in bed for the rest of the day. He was kind and solicitous and insisted it was his fault. He brought her magazines and fruit and instructed Maggie to rub in some linament.

It smelled foul and Holly wrinkled her nose at him the next time he came to see her. 'Is this what you use on your horses?'

His chuckle was sensuous, his dark eyes warm and friendly. He bent low and kissed her lightly on the lips. 'You smell adorable, my sweet.'

'Only because you can't tell the difference,' she parried goodnaturedly. 'Any woman who smells like a horse or a bottle of whisky would seem good to you.'

'Not any woman, Holly. Please hurry and get better.'

She dared not ask him why, but her heart began a sudden hammering against her ribs and she found herself unable to look into his face.

He touched her cheek and his fingertips scorched. Her senses reeled and she found it difficult to breathe and retreated back into her pillow, eyes wide and apprehensive.

'You're a strange mixture.' His voice was low and seductive. 'Prickly and defensive one moment, a willing lover the next, and now—you're afraid? It doesn't make sense.'

He sat on the edge of the bed, and the weight of him made her slip fractionally nearer. 'Is it me you're frightened of, Holly, or those feelings of yours? It's my guess you've never felt this way with Steve. It's a totally new experience and you're unsure how to handle it.'

There was so much truth in his words that Holly could say nothing in her defence. She toyed with the ribbon decorating the front of her nightie, pulling the bow undone and retying it with quick nervous fingers, then beginning all over again.

With a wry smile he took her hands, folding them between his own powerful ones. 'Don't be nervous, little kitten. I mean you no harm.'

'I know,' she said huskily. 'It's just that I've never come across anyone like you before.' She ran the tip of her tongue over her lips and looked at him from beneath the long lashes which framed her beautiful eyes. 'You accuse me of being changeable, but you're no better yourself. You were so hateful when we first met that I loathed you on sight.'

'That was before I got to know you,' he said gruffly. He stroked the back of her hand and she looked at the long lean fingers with their square well-manicured nails. There were dark hairs lying against the bronzed skin, veins showing faintly through.

He had taken off his sweater and wore a cream silk shirt, the cuffs rolled back to reveal strong forearms, the corded muscles indicative of many hours' hard manual work.

Without even realising what she was doing she withdrew her hand from his and ran her fingers experimentally along his arm, tracing a line from wrist to elbow, luxuriating in the feel of his hard skin beneath her fingertips.

'I'm not sure you don't still hate me?'

There were gold flecks in his eyes that Holly had never noticed before, lightening them, making them not quite so mysterious. She shook her head. 'Not any more.' She felt hypnotised, as though she was saying what he wanted her to say, and not what she really meant.

Except that it was true. There was no hate now, nothing but pure unadulterated love. She had heard someone say once that there had to be hate before you could love. She had thought it a rather stupid statement at the time. Now it turned out to be true.

'Then we have nothing to worry about,' he said, raising her hand to his mouth and kissing each of her fingers in turn.

Shivers ran up Holly's arm, entering her nerve-stream until she could think of nothing and no one but this exciting sexy man sitting on her bed.

It was the first time she had had a man in her bedroom and there was something vaguely wicked about it that made it all the more exhilarating. Many of her girl friends slept around, she knew that, but she had always had Steve and he was not that type.

It occurred to her now that Steve had never really had much interest in sexual activities. Marriage to him would have been very dull, very unsatisfying. At least she had Calum to thank for opening her eyes in that direction, even if nothing ever developed between them.

The way things were going, though, it looked as if Calum might be changing his mind about allowing no woman to enter his life. He was certainly showing a great deal of interest in her, and she would be a fool to resist, feeling about him as she did.

'I think you should rest now,' he said. 'Much as I

hate leaving you I have work to do. One of those new Ayrshires isn't settling down as she ought, and I want to take another look at Lady, just in case. I'll come in to say goodnight.'

He did not kiss her again and Holly felt sad. She wanted him so much it hurt.

The next day Holly decided to get up. 'I can't lie in bed,' she explained to Maggie when the housekeeper exclaimed in horror upon finding her almost dressed. 'It will drive me mad.'

'But the laird left instructions,' protested the woman. 'I've brought your breakfast. He won't take kindly to you——'

'I know,' interrupted Holly. 'He told me the same thing. I'm afraid I'm not very good at obeying orders. I feel a bit sore and stiff but it's probably because I've not ridden in years.'

Maggie looked out of sorts, the folds of her face hanging down in disapproval, her button eyes cold with their usual hostility. 'So long as he doesn't blame me.'

'I'll make sure of that,' said Holly, 'and thank you for pressing my clothes. I'm very grateful.'

The woman sniffed and went out of the room still carrying the tray she had come in with. 'I'll put this in the breakfast room,' she announced. 'Some people have no consideration. As if I haven't enough to do without running around after ungrateful lassies.'

Her voice faded as she reached the stairs and Holly gave a resigned shrug and finished dressing. She had chosen a white peasant blouse with rich embroidery, and a red skirt that was both cheerful and pretty. Her hip did ache but not so much that she could not walk. The linament, whether it was meant for horses or not, had evidently done the trick.

She ate a leisurely breakfast, glancing through the newspaper that Calum had left earlier, wondering whether he would put in an appearance later or if his work would keep him busy for the rest of the day.

She hoped not. In the light of their new relationship every minute spent away from him seemed like an hour. Last night she had been asleep before he returned and now she could not wait to see him again.

In the event it was early evening before he put in an appearance and Holly was feeling distinctly neglected and out of sorts. It did not help when he said brusquely, 'What are you doing out of bed? I distinctly left instructions that you were to stay there for the whole day.'

She jutted her chin characteristically. 'I make up my own mind, thank you. And in case you think Maggie did not pass on the message, she did. Like you, she was not very pleased, but there was nothing at all she could do about it.'

'If I'd been here I'd have made damn certain you never moved,' he growled. 'How are you?'

'As if you care,' threw Holly furiously, wondering what had happened to the tender compassionate man of the day before.

'Would I ask if I didn't?' he snapped. 'Really, Holly, you're behaving irrationally.'

'Considering that you haven't had the common decency to spare one minute of your time today to enquire after my health, I think I'm entitled to,' Holly retorted, stung by his arrogance.

He eyed her coldly. 'Is that what you think? It hasn't occurred to your selfish little mind that I might have had an emergency on my hands and couldn't get away even though I wanted to?'

Holly began to feel guilty. It looked as though she had been making a fuss when his absence could not be helped. She was behaving like a wife!

'I didn't know,' she said quietly. 'Is it Lady?' She felt cold all of a sudden. If anything had happened to the horse it would be her fault.

Calum shook his head. 'It's that cow. We've had to put her down.' He thrust his hand roughly through his hair, his face deeply etched with lines of strain and worry. 'She caught her udder on some wire, tore it right across. We've worked all day trying to save her, but the poor thing was in such agony it was kinder to put her to sleep.'

'How awful,' cried Holly at once, her brow furrowed at the mere thought of such a thing. 'How did it happen?'

He sighed. 'I'm not sure. Duncan put up a temporary fence to divide that big field, if you remember. It looked to me as though the cow had tried to jump it. We found her lying there this morning bleeding like a stuck pig.' He poured himself a glass of whisky and took a long swallow before looking at her again. His eyes were ringed with fatigue and Holly had never seen him look so sad.

'I wish there was something I could say,' she said.

He grimaced. 'You could pretend to be pleased to see me, instead of spoiling for an argument.'

She thought it best not to mention that it was he who had started it. 'I am, Calum,' she said quietly. 'It's been a long day.'

'For me too,' he sighed, 'and the last thing I want now is to have words with you. I need rest and good company, and I'm starving.'

Holly pushed herself up and walked towards him,

trying not to give away the fact that her bottom was sore from riding, or that her hip was more painful now than it had been when she had got up that morning. She caught his arm and smiled up into his face. 'I think dinner's ready. Shall we go in?'

It was a day or two before Calum would let Holly go back to work, even though she declared that she was perfectly capable of sitting at a desk and typing a few letters. He treated her as though she was something fragile and although Holly yearned for something more satisfying out of their relationship, it was nevertheless comforting to have him so concerned.

Then one morning he suggested they make their postponed visit to the distillery. 'I think, though,' he said, 'we'll go by car. It might be safer.'

'Does that mean you're not ever going to let me ride again?'

He grinned. 'It means I value the safety of my horses.'

'But you couldn't care less about me?' There was an impish smile on her lips and her eyes danced as she looked him boldly in the eye. It was really extraordinary how they had stopped hating each other and could now banter quite successfully with no offence being taken by either side.

'You're not my property,' he said unexpectedly.

This did cause Holly to jerk her head and look at him quizzically. 'May I be permitted to ask what that means?'

'It's elementary, my dear girl,' came the bland reply. 'Don't tell me you've forgotten all about poor unfortunate Steve? You sent him away with a flea in his ear and I'm sure he must be lamenting the day you met me. Have you phoned him recently, or are you letting him suffer a little while longer?'

This was the Calum she did not like, the side of him she had not seen for a long time, and Holly was suddenly on the defensive. 'That's my business,' she said, and wondered why she felt guilty. She wished he had not mentioned him. She had been doing her best to push Steve from her mind. One day soon she supposed she would have to tell him that she did not want to marry him, but she was hoping her silence would do it for her. If the truth was known she was taking the coward's way out. She liked him, even if she did not love him, and she did not want to see him hurt.

'I have no wish to make it mine,' he returned evenly. 'Shall we go?'

It was the first time she had been inside a car with Calum and she could not help thinking that sitting on horseback suited him better. Not that he could not handle the vehicle, he was as expert at that as everything else, but she gained the impression that he was much happier with a live, sometimes unpredictable, animal at his command, even though the car was very new and very smart.

It smelled of leather and was automatic so that he had very little work to do. His hands held the wheel lightly and she found her eyes drawn to them, remembering the time when he had explored her body and she had forgotten all about her aches and pains.

He had never attempted to make love to her again. She wondered whether he regretted it or whether he was waiting until she had fully recovered. It was a tantalising thought and one which occupied her for most of the short journey to his whisky distillery.

It came as a surprise when they rounded a bend in the road and suddenly, in the middle of the grandeur and majesty of the Scottish Highlands they came upon a cluster of white buildings that were so well hidden they detracted not one bit from their splendid surroundings.

Holly was introduced to the manager, a big burly man with the brightest red hair she had ever seen and blue eyes that took their time in looking over the English girl who was the unexpected companion of the laird. She could almost guess what he was thinking, and she had an idea that she was the only woman Calum had ever taken to the distillery.

She had never really given any thought as to how whisky was made and listened attentively as Calum explained how the barley had first to be malted.

'Do you grow your own?' she asked.

'Oh yes,' he said at once. 'Naturally if we expand we would have to buy it in, probably from England, and more than likely ready-malted. But for the moment we grow and malt our own.'

She discovered that to malt barley the grains were soaked for several days in tanks of water called steeps, then it was spread on the malting floor to germinate, and turned at frequent intervals. 'This takes between eight and twelve days,' explained Calum. 'It secretes an enzyme which makes the starch in the barley soluble and prepares it for turning into sugar.'

After that it went into a kiln for drying and Calum told her that the smoke from the peat fire at the base of the kiln was drawn up through an open ventilator at the top. 'It is what gives the whisky its smokey flavour,' he added. 'I saw you looking at the ventilator when we drove up—the one like a pagoda. All distilleries have those distinctive shaped heads.'

'I'm glad you told me,' she laughed. 'I thought I must be seeing things.'

He took her hand and they watched as the malt, which the barley had now become, was released from its storage bins into a dressing machine where it was cleaned, weighed, then passed through to the mill where it was ground.

Holly found it all very interesting and asked countless questions as they passed from one operation to another. She discovered that the spent grain, called draff, was used as winter food for the cattle so there was absolutely no waste at all.

She was surprised to see the whisky was clear when it was piped into the casks, but discovered that it had to be matured for three years at least before it could be bottled, during which time it gradually turned to golden brown.

'Some whisky is matured for fifteen years or more,' informed Calum. 'What happens is that air enters the casks and evaporation takes place. Eventually the whisky loses its coarseness and becomes smooth and mellow. Even this,' he continued, indicating the rows of casks, 'is not the end of the road. Some of it will be bottled as single whisky, but the rest will be sent to the blenders and there could be as many as forty single whiskies blended together.'

By the time they were back in the car Holly knew a lot more than she had before setting out, she also felt that her relationship with Calum had taken another step forward. Throughout the whole tour he had treated her with a warmth she could not ignore, and now her senses were attuned to such a fine degree that she tingled all over, and was more than ever aware of his sexual magnetism.

She already knew what it felt like to be in his arms, but it seemed that he did not even need to touch her for her to respond. There was a compelling maleness about him that elated her, that caused her to react in a manner that had hitherto been alien to her nature.

Risking a glance she took in once again those noble, arrogant features, the smooth high brow, that long nose and tough jawline, those sensuous lips that could arouse the most basic feelings.

The depth of her emotions frightened her. She had always been so proud that she never let herself get carried away, yet here was this man, a comparative stranger, whom she found impossible to resist.

He looked at her and smiled and covered her hand with his own. His touch did alarming things to her senses and she turned quickly away.

'I'm glad you've recovered,' he said, a wealth of meaning behind his tone.

Holly would have had to be stupid not to know what he meant and her pulses raced crazily, the blood pounding in her head. If it had not meant admitting that he disturbed her she would have pulled her hand away.

'Me too,' she said. 'I hate being inactive. That's one of the things I miss up here. I used to play badminton and squash regularly. It kept me fit.'

'And very trim, if I may say so,' he smiled. 'There's always riding, of course, if your fall hasn't unnerved you? I go out early every morning. You're quite welcome to join me.'

Holly felt she was progressing by leaps and bounds. Considering how inhospitable he had been when she first arrived in the glen, he was certainly making up for it now.

'I might do that,' she said, trying not to sound too eager.

'And then there's the pool. I seem to remember you have a penchant for nude swimming?' He glanced at her wickedly and there was something in his eyes that suggested he was seeing her naked now.

Holly felt her cheeks colour and threw him a swift deprecating look. 'I don't find that amusing.'

He chuckled, again that deep sensuous sound that sent her nerves skittering. 'Neither do I. Interesting is the word I would use. How about it? We should have time for a quick dip before lunch.'

She had not thought he was serious, now she eyed him speculatively. 'You don't mean that?'

'Indeed I do.' He let go of her hand to negotiate the car round a series of hairpin bends.

Holly twisted her fingers tightly together and felt every muscle in her stomach knot. It was a heady thought, but not very practical. 'I've not brought my bikini with me, so I'm afraid the answer must be no.'

'Coward!' he mocked. 'Who are you afraid of, me? I'm sure you wouldn't be so prudish if it were your boyfriend.'

At the mention of Steve Holly again felt guilty. It was wrong to be enjoying herself so much with another man. 'Steve would not even suggest it,' she said tightly.

'Then Steve is even more of a fool than he's so far proved,' he returned equably. 'Come on, lass, what's happened to your sense of adventure? If it really does go against the grain you can wear your bra and pants. I appreciate your desire to preserve your modesty.'

His lips curled upwards at the corners and although he was not looking at her Holly knew exactly what pictures were passing through his mind's eye. 'I've decided I still hate you,' she said without conviction.

'I'm sure you do.' Calum experienced difficulty in controlling his amusement. 'But you're coming swimming all the same. Isn't that right?'

How could she resist him? There was something about this man that defied opposition. She guessed no one ever refused him anything, especially a woman. 'I suppose so. You don't seem to be prepared to take no for an answer. Are you always so insistent?'

'When it's something I want,' he said, the deep timbre of his voice reflecting an emotion she preferred not to notice.

She was becoming more deeply involved with every day that passed, and the fact that she was at Shilda House for the sole purpose of discovering whether her grandfather really had lost Braeside over a game of poker was fading ever further into the background. In fact she scarcely thought about it. All she did think about was her obsession for Calum. It was so strong as to be unreal and absolutely without purpose. For where could it all end?

Calum was using her, he had to be. He had vowed to remain a bachelor all his life. Unless—he was slowly changing his mind? He had certainly changed in his attitude towards her, and she preferred to believe that it was genuine affection and not simple lust. It had to be. If all he wanted was her body he would not show her the consideration he had during her enforced rest. There had to be more to it than lascivious desire.

The pool was little more than half a mile from Shilda House, so after they had collected towels they decided to walk.

Water frothed down the steep side of the mountain to form a large natural pool, before continuing on its course to feed the river. It was crystal clear and reputedly bottomless, although Holly had her doubts about that. She had believed it as a child, naturally, but now treated the legend with the scepticism she felt it deserved.

Calum unselfconsciously began to undress and she watched in fascination as he removed his shirt. His chest was as broad as she had imagined. It was also smooth and golden and as he moved the skin rippled like silk over hard muscles. She had an urge to touch him, to run her fingers over that deep tan, feel the hidden power.

When he unbuckled his belt and peeled off his trousers, she knew the polite thing would be to turn her head, but there was something hypnotic about watching this man perform. Her eyes were drawn to the narrow hips and long length of powerful thigh, to the skin-tight black trunks and the flat firm stomach.

He was easily the most exciting male animal she had ever seen and she was overcome by his sheer primitiveness, her pulses leaping in response so that she quite forgot she was supposed to be getting undressed too.

'I take it you are going to join me?'

The sardonic question brought her back to her senses and she looked at him nervously from beneath her lashes. 'In a moment.'

'You mean you expect me to turn my back and spare your blushes?' he grinned. 'Why should I when you've enjoyed yourself watching me?'

Not realising he had observed her appraisal Holly for once did not know what to say. He must think her frightfully naïve, as though she had never seen a man undress before.

He laughed at her discomfiture then turned and

executed a perfect dive into the glittering water. When he surfaced he began to swim strongly away from her and Holly took the opportunity to slip out of her skirt and blouse. She stepped warily over the moss-covered stones at the edge and slid into the water quietly so as not to draw attention to herself.

But she had underestimated its coldness. Calum had given no clue that it was not so warm as it looked and the icy temperature took her breath away so that she gasped and cried out, wrapping her arms about her shoulders, trying to stop her teeth from chattering.

She decided this was not for her and was about to haul herself out when Calum appeared at her side. 'Why didn't you tell me it was like this?' she demanded.

'You should know,' he said, eyes glinting wickedly, his black hair plastered to his well-shaped head. 'You've done it before.'

'You don't feel the cold when you're a kid,' she cried. 'This is ridiculous. I'm getting out before I end up with pneumonia.'

His brows rose smoothly. 'Where are those guts I so admire? Don't tell me you're going soft.' He disappeared beneath the water and the next second she felt a grip on her ankles. She just had time to draw breath before he pulled her down.

A few seconds fighting with Calum made her forget the cold, and when he finally let her go she discovered she had got used to it, the water no longer felt like ice. Instead it felt silky smooth against her body, stimulating her senses, making her even more aware of Calum's intoxicating virility.

Those few moments spent against him, feeling the firmness of his thighs against her own, a powerful leg pushed between hers, an arm brushing her breasts, had woken all her basic instincts, making her decide that there was something very erotic indeed about a man's naked body oiled by sweet natural spring water.

She challenged him to a race but was not surprised when she lost. Her super-charged emotions made her incapable of using her full strength. She felt as weak as a kitten and about as defenceless, and was relieved when he decided they had had enough.

He climbed out first, then held his hand down to help her. He lifted her effortlessly, only the tightening muscles in his arms revealing that he had to put any strength into the action.

She expected him to let her go, instead he took both her hands and held her away from him. 'Let me look at you,' he said thickly, and then, 'God, you're beautiful!'

His eyes ravaged her, stripping her, taking in every detail of her green luminous eyes, her trembling lips, and that rapid pulse at the base of her throat that always gave her away.

Suddenly shy, Holly looked demurely down, needing to avoid the hot desire in his eyes. Not until that moment did she realise that her bra and pants had become transparent. With a strangled cry of embarrassment she turned away, but his grip tightened and she was his prisoner whether she liked it or not.

Her breathing deepened and he did not miss the rapid rise and fall of her breasts, blatantly lingering before moving his gaze downwards over the flatness of her stomach and her gently rounded hips. Holly felt naked and vulnerable and tried to ignore the clawing ache in her stomach.

When with a groan he pulled her to him, she

experienced a thrill of sheer pagan pleasure at the feel of his cold damp body against hers. Her breasts were crushed against the solid wall of his chest and she felt every inch of his hard-boned thighs.

There was something barbarous and beautiful about standing in that ferny paradise, the warm summer sun filtering prettily through the trees. She felt an entirely different person. As though she did not belong to herself any more. She was Calum's. He had brought her to this magical place and woven his spell over her so that she was his to do with as he wanted.

When their lips met it was a mutual decision. Holly offered herself freely, her arms snaking round the back of his neck. His mouth tasted cold and sweet and entirely sensuous—and time stood still.

He moulded her body to his, his hands moving intimately over her, the pressure of his lips increasing until her mouth opened willingly.

As his tongue explored and tasted the inviting moistness of her mouth she felt treacherous flames of desire sear her limbs and although she knew she ought to fight, that somewhere in all this she ought to think about Steve and put this man from her, she was putty in his hands.

She made a token gesture of denial. 'Please, Calum . . .'

'Please what?' he mocked. 'Please you want this as much as me?' His mouth once again fastened on hers with a savage intensity that drew a throbbing response.

Holly found herself completely unable to resist. If this was love, then what she had felt for Steve was nothing. Never had she felt the rapturous delight she experienced now. It ran through her veins like liquid fire causing her to arch herself even closer so that she could feel every bone in his body pressing into her. She was in danger of drowning in her own hedonistic desires.

'This is all wrong,' she managed to husk when his mouth left hers to burn a trail down the slim column of her throat.

'Why is it wrong when it is what we both want?' he asked thickly, pausing a moment to glance at her. There was a glazed look to his eyes that Holly had never seen before. It both scared and excited her and she knew she ought to back out before it was too late. But how could she when she needed him so badly? When she was almost frantic with a longing that matched his?

'Steve,' she murmured weakly.

'To hell with Steve,' he choked. 'He's had his chance. You're not surely trying to tell me that you prefer that milksop?' He looked angry all of a sudden, his arms tightening round her body until she felt he must surely crush her.

She shook her head, immune to the pain he was inflicting, blind to everything except her own need of him. Their surroundings had faded into a hazy blur. There was just herself and Calum and a love that was threatening her sanity.

His lips were on hers again, his hands sliding over her back, unclasping her bra and then swinging her into his arms to lay her down on the bed of ferns, stretching his long length on top of her, their lips still locked in a kiss that promised eternity.

'Oh, Holly,' he mouthed brokenly, when at last he drew back and looked at her. 'You're so beautiful, so desirable.' He cupped her aching breasts, teasing her nipples until she cried out at the exquisite torture.

She found it increasingly difficult to breathe and could only look at him with eyes full of pain and adoration. She could hide her feelings no longer. She reached up and touched his face, ran her fingers along the strong jutting line of his jaw, explored the chiselled outline of his lips.

He traced the outline of her fingers with his tongue, every stroke sensuous and erotic. Holly's head spun and she felt as though she was going to pass out with sheer pleasure. She closed her eyes and then felt his weight on her again.

She moved her hands across the bare skin of his back. It was as soft as silk yet sheathed a muscled hardness that could not be denied. He was powerful and strong, and expert in the art of making a woman feel as though she was losing her senses. Her brain had dulled and she could think of nothing except her love for him, her need of him, the aching that filled every quivering nerve.

'Oh, God, I want you,' he murmured hoarsely against her mouth. 'You know that, don't you?'

She nodded dumbly, what could she say? It must surely be obvious in her every move.

'You don't mind?' The question hung in the air above them.

Again a mute shake of her head. She could smell damp peat and the animal odour of Calum's body, she could hear the music of running water, and the sound of bells in her head that were perhaps a warning, but which she chose to ignore.

'And you want me?' His voice had grown harsher and deeper and it was as though he, too, had difficulty in breathing.

Holly could not answer. It seemed somehow

disloyal to Steve, even, though she knew it was too late. She had already gone past the point when she could go back to him.

'Say it, damn you!' Calum sounded suddenly angry. 'I want to hear you say it.'

She swallowed a lump as big as a golf ball in her throat and looked at him with wide moist eyes, pleading with him to understand. She not only wanted him, she loved him, and she wanted to hear him say that he loved her. She did not want him to take her simply because he found her desirable. If that was his sole purpose, then all this was wrong. 'Wh—why—do you—want me?'

'Why?' he echoed. 'What a bloody stupid question. Why does a man ever want a woman? God, Holly, don't tell me you've driven me this far to back out?'

She ran her tongue over her trembling lips. 'I thought that you—you—I——' She stopped and shook her head, balking at the word loved, trying to hang on to her last shred of pride. She couldn't say it. No man, especially someone like Calum, liked to be taken for granted.

But he was one step ahead. 'That I what?' There was a look of positive disbelief on his face. 'That I *love* you? For pity's sake, Holly, have some sense. You're going to marry Steve—or so you tell me. This is nothing more than a pleasant interlude. It's what you want, isn't it?'

She shook her head, rolling it from side to side, feeling the bracken claw at her hair. 'No!' she cried shrilly. 'Not like this, not ever!' She clapped her hands to her face and refused to look at him. 'Go away! *Please*, go away!'

He swore and snatched at her hands, and she

flinched at the cold hardness in his eyes. It was impossible to believe that seconds earlier they had been filled with desire, that he had been as overcome by his emotions as she herself. Now he was in complete and utter control. 'You're not trying to tell me that you—*imagined*—you were in love with me? That that was the reason why you offered yourself so willingly?' His tone was scathing, cutting through Holly as physically as if he had used a knife.

She buried the palms of her hands in her eyeballs. God, why had she been so transparent? How would she ever be able to face him again?

'I take it you're not going to answer?' He pushed himself up and she shivered and crossed her hands over her naked breasts, though what privacy that could afford her she did not know. She had committed the unforgivable crime of baring her soul—and to a man who found sadistic pleasure in crushing her heart and throwing it back, treating it with the contempt he thought it deserved.

It was an effort to pull herself together, but somehow she managed it. She too rose to her feet, picking up her skirt and holding it defensively in front of her, eyeing him with what she hoped was icy disdain.

'Oh, yes, I'll give you your answer,' she said, and was surprised to hear how steady her voice sounded. 'Very foolishly I did imagine that I was in love with you. But I see it now for what it was. It was simply hate in another guise. You excite me, Calum, I'll admit that. Arousing a woman is something at which you are very expert. In my naïvety I mistook my feelings. I thought that my first impressions of you were wrong, I was quite prepared to admit that I had misjudged you.

'Now I see that you're every bit the bastard you were when we first met. I hate you, Calum, from the bottom of my heart, and I hope I shall never have the misfortune to see you again.'

CHAPTER EIGHT

AFTER Holly had finished her speech Calum stared at her for several long, tense, emotion-filled seconds. She prayed he would go. She did not feel she could hold out much longer. All she wanted was to crumple into a heap and sob her heart out.

As if from a distance she finally heard him speak. 'Thank you, Holly, for being honest. Now perhaps you'll let me say what I think of a girl who belongs to one man and flings herself unashamedly at another. At one time I felt sorry for you, I thought you were throwing your life away.'

He paused, looking at her coldly as if expecting her to interrupt. When she merely returned his gaze without flinching, without revealing that she was being slowly destroyed, he continued, 'Now it is Steve I feel sorry for, being saddled with a hypocritical little bitch like you. What would he say, I wonder, if he knew how shamelessly you had offered yourself to me? Do you think he'd have you back? Perhaps I ought to tell him? I should hate to see a fellow man destroy his life because he loves a woman who is not worthy of him.'

As she now had no intention of marrying Steve none of this should have had any effect on her. Unfortunately it made her feel like the lowest of the low, and she waited only for the moment he would tire of preaching and leave her to sort herself out. When it became evident that he expected some sort of response she said tiredly. 'Steve, thank goodness, is not like you. He will understand that I could not help myself. He knows what type of a man you are.'

'So you do still plan on marrying the poor guy?'

Holly tossed her head and held the red skirt closer. 'I see no reason why not.' It was best he thought that way.

'He has my sympathies.' Calum tugged on his socks and trousers over damp skin, scorning the towel, impatient now, she guessed, to be gone. He did not even bother with his shirt, snatching it from the ground and trailing it carelessly as he strode away.

It was not until he had disappeared that Holly realised how cold she was. Even after she had rubbed herself dry and dragged on her clothes she could not control her shivering limbs. She had brought a clean set of undies to the pool and she wrapped the others in the towel, intending to get rid of them as soon as possible. She would never be able to wear them again without thinking of Calum desecrating her body.

Even now she could feel his long-fingered hands on her breasts, his possessive lips against hers, and she cried aloud in anguish. What a cheap fool she had been. Why had she ever imagined that he might return her love? Why hadn't she realised that the likes of Calum McEwan did not love their women? They took what was offered, they seduced and manipulated so cleverly that most girls could not see through them until it was too late. Thank goodness she had come to her senses in time.

Her feet felt like lead as she made her way back eventually to Shilda House. She went straight up to her room, keeping her fingers mentally crossed that she would not meet Calum. But the house was like a morgue. She was worrying for nothing.

With shaking hands she thrust her clothes into her suitcases. Steve's packing was perfection compared to this. She heaved them downstairs and outside to the garage where Calum had stabled her car. The key, fortunately, was in the ignition. She had not relished the idea of having to ask.

It was not until she was actually inside the cottage that she felt able to let go. She sat down in her grandfather's favourite chair and allowed her tears to take over. Gradually she felt better and with her returning strength came a determination to show the laird that she was not without guts.

He probably thought that after their showdown she would leave the glen and never return. But that would be the easy way out. There was still the matter of the ownership of this cottage to be proved and it would give her great pleasure to be able to tell him it was hers.

But first of all she had to get herself sorted out. She lit a fire, sitting a kettle of water on it to boil while she hung away her clothes. After two cups of tea she felt better and it dawned on her exactly what a state she was in as she remembered that the electricity had been put back on and she could have boiled the electric kettle without any of this fuss.

Laughter at her own stupidity restored her sense of humour and with it the realisation that her stomach was clamouring for food. She heated a tin of soup and ate it with the last of the crackers, which were by now stale and tasteless, and decided to go into Invercray and do some shopping.

It was not until a quick glance at her watch told her it was almost five that she knew she was too late to do anything about it today. It would have to be something else out of a tin for supper, and then first thing in the morning into town to restock her pantry.

There was also a good chance that she would be able to ferret out some information concerning her grandparents. They had lived here all their lives and were well-known in the small town. It should be relatively simple finding out whether anyone knew about that important game of poker.

When she heard a vehicle she thought at first it was Calum come to order her out and her heart-beats quickened as she opened the door. But the man who confronted her was a stranger. It was clear by his words, though, that he knew her.

'I'd like a word with ye, Miss Burns. May I come in?'

He did not sound particularly friendly and Holly hesitated. She was not so sure that she liked the look of this man with the sharp nose and inquisitive eyes. He wore a tartan kilt and a woollen shirt and he held himself proud and erect, almost as though he were the laird. Except that he had none of Calum's height and breadth, and his grey hair was thinning fast.

'What is it that you want to see me about?' she asked defensively, her chin lifting, her brilliant eyes searching his face.

'I think it would be best discussed inside,' he said, and without waiting for her to speak again he pushed past her and strode into the sitting room.

He stood, as had Calum, with his back to the fire, his legs apart, his cold pale eyes watching her with an insolence that Holly resented. 'Suppose you tell me who you are?' she said strongly. 'This does happen to be my cottage and I'm afraid I find your intrusion very annoying.'

'The name's Duncan Gillies,' he said stiffly—and awaited her reaction.

'I see,' was all she allowed him. So this was Calum's factor! The man he swore was his right hand, who could run the estate single-handed if necessary. And now Calum was using his henchman to get rid of her! Too cowardly to do the job himself.

He was not at all what she had expected. The way Calum had sung his praises she had pictured someone resembling Calum himself. Not this puny-looking individual who would do better to hide his legs inside a pair of trousers than display their stick-like structure beneath a kilt. The only powerful thing about him was his eyes, and even they were a pale insipid blue as though someone had dabbed them with a paintbrush that was almost dry. She judged him to be in his mid-sixties and his face was hard and leathery, covered with a network of wrinkles.

'Ye are aware of my position on the laird's estate?'

'Oh, yes,' she said, and waited for him to carry on.

For a second he seemed nonplussed by her apparent indifference to his rank. Then he said in a voice that was deep with emotion. 'Ye are not wanted here, Miss Burns. Do yourself a favour and pack your bags and go.'

'Mr McEwen sent you to tell me that, I suppose?' Holly's voice was as cold as the factor's.

'The laird has nothing at all to do with this.' There was an aggressive tilt to the man's head that made Holly dislike him even more. For a little man he was acting very big.

'Then exactly why are you here, Mr Gillies?' For some inexplicable reason Holly felt that things could turn out to be very unpleasant and wished she had never allowed him inside. He was the meanest-looking individual she had ever seen and she could not imagine why Calum should think so highly of him.

He began pacing up and down the room. 'I was very disconcerted when I discovered the laird's change of plan. Miss Drummond was an eminently suitable young lady, I can't think why he should have preferred you, and the fact that he allowed you to live at the house is extraordinary after the trouble he has had in the past.'

'And is that any business of yours?' asked Holly, wondering who the hell this man thought he was.

'I like to think that I am looking after the laird's interests,' he said, shooting her a glance that was so full of hate and venom that Holly felt as if a cold hand had clutched at her stomach.

'I think Mr McEwen can look after himself.' Her tone was as icy as his. 'And I'm quite sure he would not thank you for interfering. If that's all you've come for then I suggest you leave. I have no wish to discuss my affairs with you.' She was shocked to discover she was trembling and forced herself to breathe deeply and slowly, clenching her hands behind her back so that this horrible little man should not see the effect he was having on her.

Duncan Gillie's thin upper lip curled, revealing a row of tobacco-stained teeth. 'What happens on this estate is very much my business. I've worked for the McEwens all my life, my father and grandfather before me. Their business is my business and I do not like to see the young laird making a fool of himself.'

Holly felt faintly amused by this ambiguous statement. Calum McEwen would never do that. 'Calum is perfectly capable of making his own decisions.'

'Some men,' he said bitterly, 'cannot help themselves when there is a pretty young lady involved. I must say you're not quite what I expected, but then it would be your very innocence that would appeal to the laird. He would not realise how cleverly you were twisting him round your little finger.'

'Mr Gillies,' said Holly heatedly, 'you've said enough. I refuse to stand here and listen to your pathetic accusations. Please go.'

But the pale eyes continued to relentlessly probe her face, as if trying to see for himself what exceptional qualities she possessed. 'Your riding accident was a master stroke. You really had him going then. Perhaps I should congratulate you?'

'He told you about it—or were you spying on us?' shot Holly accusingly, suddenly wondering whether it was this man's hostility she had felt when first coming to the glen, not Calum's. It was certainly so powerful that it was eating into him, destroying him, making him a very dangerous enemy.

His high forehead creased into hundreds of wrinkles as he slid his straggly brows up, the washed-out eyes widening so that they were as round as pebbles, the pupils dilating as he gazed intently at her. There was something hypnotic about them and Holly found that she could not look away.

'I've seen you with him,' he admitted.

Holly went hot, wondering whether he had observed them at the pool. It occurred to her that this man could be a sex maniac. Perhaps he had seen their love-play and now thought that he could . . . The idea sickened her even as yet again she was relieved that she had had the foresight to do that judo training. She had never imagined she would need it here in

Scotland, but it showed how wrong you could be. 'I think you're despicable,' she shot, lifting her chin and eyeing him warily. 'What Calum does has nothing at all to do with you.'

The fierce eyes never moved from her face. 'Since your arrival the laird has behaved irrationally. I have never, *never*, known him take a woman to the distillery. It is one of his unwritten rules not to mix business with pleasure. Quite how you managed to change him I don't know, but let me say I am relieved he has had the good sense to kick you out of his house. All that remains now is for you to leave the glen altogether.' He folded his arms across his narrow chest and stood with one foot slightly forward, his chin thrust aggressively.

It was comforting to know that he was not after her body but she was damn sure she was not going to let him order her out of her own cottage. Calum had not managed it and this little apology for a man stood no chance at all. He might be manager of the estate, but he did not manage her.

'Let's get things straight, Mr Gillies,' she said. 'First of all, Calum did not kick me out of his house, I left of my own accord. Secondly, this cottage belongs to me and no one, and most certainly not you, will force me to leave it. Is that understood?' She really could do with sitting down. Her legs felt most unusually weak and her heart was hammering like a mad thing in her breast.

The sharp nose twitched, like a ferret sniffing out a rat. 'Correction, Miss Burns. Braeside belongs to the estate.'

'Really?' she returned haughtily. 'On what assumption do you make your claim?'

'Not assumption, I assure you. It is public knowledge that Alasdair Burns lost this cottage over a game of cards.'

'Is that a fact?' Holly had the strangest feeling that she was losing her battle. 'Can you show me proof?'

He looked indignant. 'What more proof do ye want than a man's word? James McEwen told the story so many times that I doubt there's not one person who hasnae heard it.'

'But supposing it wasn't true?' argued Holly. 'Who's to say he wasn't drunk at the time and the whole thing was a figment of his imagination? I'm sure that if my grandfather had been so foolish as to wager this cottage he would have been the first to admit that it was no longer his. He left it to me in his will. Therefore I am confident that it still legally belonged to him, and I'm going to fight tooth and nail to prove it.'

There was an instant of shock on his face following Holly's outburst. Quite clearly he had not expected to find her so stubborn. But it was gone immediately. 'You'd be wasting your time. You'd do as well to get out now and save all the unpleasantries.'

'So far as I can see it's you who is being unpleasant, Mr Gillies.' Holly had never felt so coldly angry. 'And if you think that Mr McEwen will approve of your bully-boy tactics you have a misguided sense of loyalty. I'd be careful if I were you. I might just take it into my head to tell him what you are up to.'

A nervous tic appeared beneath one eye, but his aggression did not lessen. 'I mean what I say, Miss Burns. I want you out of this cottage. You're a disruptive influence in the laird's life. I am thinking only of him. I'll give you until in the morning to make up your mind.'

'And when you find me still here what will you do then?' Holly stared at him arrogantly.

He returned her gaze unflinchingly. 'There are other ways of making you leave. Good day, Miss Burns. I do hope you will be sensible.'

Not until the door closed behind him did Holly allow herself the pleasure of sitting down. She felt physically drained and wondered what she had done to deserve this hassle. She had certainly not expected it. Her memories of Glen Shilda were that it was the most peaceful place on earth. Instead she had found hostility and hatred, and silent resentment. It made her wonder whether it really was worth the fight.

How long she sat there she did not know, going over and over the things Duncan Gillies had said, wondering what made him think he had the right to speak to her in such a fashion. She was quite sure that Calum did not know, nor would he be very pleased if he found out. Calum was capable of doing his own dirty work.

She wished now that she had not allowed her love for Calum to blind her to everything else. All those days spent in the office typing out letters and entering figures in ledgers could have been more profitably spent trying to prove the cottage belonged to her.

Her lips were grim when she finally made herself get up. She felt as though the whole world was against her, and that the weight was too heavy for her young shoulders to bear. She almost wished she could put all this behind her and go back to her calmly ordered life with Steve.

But it was a fact that you could never put the clock back. Even if she gave up the whole idea of staying, letting Calum or Duncan or both feel that they had won, things would never be the same.

Calum had ruined her for Steve. He had given her a taste of what a truly exciting sexual relationship could be like. Add to that an understanding, a caring, and a friendship, and you had the recipe for genuine love.

Steve could give her these last ingredients, but did not have the spark to arouse her physically. With Calum it was the other way round, although she had thought for a while that things were different. He had definitely changed towards her, in fact he had shown considerable concern when she had hurt her hip, becoming so friendly that she felt she could be excused for making a mistake.

It was a pity that all he had wanted out of the affair was the fulfilment of his own natural urges, but it was fortunate she had discovered exactly what he was after before committing herself.

For supper she opened a tin of stewed steak, carrots and new potatoes, and although she was not conscious of feeling hungry managed to eat most of it.

By the time she made her way up to bed her resolve to fight Calum and Duncan had stiffened. No man on earth was going to do her out of what was rightfully hers. Whether she sold afterwards was another thing. It was a matter of principal. And since the fight had started there was no backing out.

The next morning Holly deliberated over whether to go into Invercray and do her shopping or wait for Duncan's visit first. In the end she stayed, deciding that if she was out he might think she had left altogether and force his way inside, maybe even changing the lock again.

But it was a nerve-racking experience and when lunch-time arrived and he had not put in an appearance she realised that she could have gone shopping after all. She decided to eat, and then if he had still not turned up she would go and risk being locked out.

'What delicacy have we on the menu today?' she asked herself as she opened the pantry door, but before she could make her choice she heard the unmistakable sound of his Land Rover.

Her heart began to bang but there was nothing on her face when she confronted him to suggest that she was in any way disturbed. She had discarded her jeans for a pretty pink summer dress and she saw the old man's mean eyes flick contemptuously over her. Although she had not dressed deliberately to impress him she knew that this was what he thought.

This time she had no intention of allowing him inside. She stood squarely in the doorway, her hands on her hips, allowing the merest hint of a smile to soften her mouth.

His legs were as spindly as ever beneath the swirling kilt, and the thin grey hair had been neatly combed over his balding head. Holly decided that he was the most repulsive man she had ever seen, and that was without taking into account his contemptible manner!

'I expected to find you gone.' The pale eyes fixed on her face.

'I'm sure you did,' she returned calmly. 'But as you can see, I'm still here, and this is where I'm going to stay, so there's nothing at all you can do about it.'

'We shall see about that.' A fanatical light appeared in his strange eyes. 'Before I've finished you'll be regretting the day you ever came to Glen Shilda. You mark my words.'

Before Holly could say anything else he had swung himself back up into the Land Rover. The engine roared as he turned in an arc and disappeared in a cloud of dust along the gravelly track.

The threat left Holly feeling shaken. Duncan Gillies was not the type of person you could ignore, even though she would have liked above all else to push him out of her mind. In his own way he had made as much of an impression on her as had Calum.

Calum! She did not really want to think about him either, yet somehow his picture image kept projecting itself into her mind. She wondered if she had been too virtuous. It was what she had wanted—more than she had wanted anything in her whole life.

She sighed and decided she had done the right thing. She had to live with herself after all, and it had always been her ambition to remain a virgin until she married. Not a very easy thing to do these days, but with Steve she had been safe. With Calum, if she had spent any more time in his company, it would have been impossible.

Not feeling in the least hungry now she gathered up her bag and keys, and after making sure the cottage was secure headed her car out of the glen towards Invercray.

The road took her alongside the bank of the loch and she stopped for a moment. There was something soothing about the calm water, about the brown trout who slid silently beneath its surface, and after a few minutes she felt more at peace.

But as she slid back into her mini she caught sight of Calum on his horse. They were quite motionless a few hundred yards along the road where she was going, and he was looking in her direction! Holly swallowed painfully and felt her pulses do all sorts of stupid things. He lifted his hand in salute and just as she debated whether she had the nerve to drive past him he galloped off into the distance and was gone.

She wondered if he thought she might be leaving, whether that wave was intended as a farewell. Bad luck for him if that was the case, she thought bitterly. He did not get rid of her that easily.

Invercray was a typical Highland town with its souvenir and antique shops, a couple of hotels, a store which sold beautiful hand-knitted garments as well as tweed and wool, a fairly new supermarket which opened during the summer months only, and a general store that had been there for years.

It was to the general store that Holly went, feeling it was unlikely anyone in the supermarket would have known her grandparents. It was very much as she remembered it, the display units more modern perhaps, but it still had those interesting smells of spice and coffee, of fruit and freshly baked bread.

Mrs Muir, behind the counter, looked as round and contented as ever, and it seemed to be the gathering place for old ladies. Holly was given an assortment of curious smiles and felt as conspicuous as a new girl at school.

'Do we know ye, dearie?' asked one old lady who was waiting to be served. 'Yer face looks familiar, yet I canna put a name to it.'

'Holly Burns,' she replied cheerfully. 'My grandparents used to live at Braeside in Glen Shilda.'

Immediately a change came over the woman's face. 'Aye, I remember them well. It's a pity ye didna put in an appearance when they were alive.' Then she turned away as though she had no more interest in the newcomer to their midst.

Their interchange had been heard by the other

customers and they all stared hostilely at Holly before whispering among themselves.

Never in her life had she felt so uncomfortable, and if she had not been so determined to find out what it was all about she would have turned tail and run.

Instead she said loudly, 'Would someone mind telling me what I am supposed to have done?' And when they were all looking at her again, 'I've come here to find out if anyone knows anything about my grandfather losing his cottage over a game of cards, not to be shunned by the lot of you.'

'If it's the cottage ye're interested in, then it's the laird ye should be asking,' said one.

'I've already spoken to Mr McEwen,' replied Holly, deciding that blunt speaking was the only way to get through to them. 'He's no help at all. He says it's his and I say it's mine. I'm trying to find out the truth. Is there no one here who can help me?'

One very prim and upright lady pursed her lips and looked at her over the top of a pair of steel-rimmed spectacles. 'It was the Burns' who needed help. Where were you when you were needed? That's the trouble with you young people today. You don't care about people. You're all self.'

Holly looked round at the circle of women. Every single one was nodding in agreement. She felt close to tears and had to swallow a sudden lump before she could defend herself. Coming on top of Duncan Gillies' treatment this was all too much. 'I haven't the slightest idea what you are talking about. I did not find out about my grandparents' deaths until after the funeral. I'd no idea they were in any kind of trouble.'

'I'm not surprised,' said Mrs Muir, speaking for the first time, 'if that high and mighty mother of yours had anything to do with it. I never met the woman but I heard about her, and that was enough. Your poor father needed his head examining, marrying a woman like her. I blame her for all that has happened. Was there anything else you were wanting, besides information? If there is I'll serve you now and you can be on your way.'

In other words, thought Holly bitterly, you'll get nothing else out of us—but they would have an awful lot to talk about when she had gone!

In fact they did not wait that long. While she was giving Mrs Muir her order Holly became aware of the mutterings going on behind her back. She strained her ears, hoping to hear what was being said. They were quick to condemn her, quick to say she should have been here, but no one was prepared to tell her why. Maggie had been the same—and if she was ever to have any peace of mind she must find out what they meant.

'It's a crying shame the way those people were neglected,' exclaimed one.

'Aye,' put in another. 'They doted on that wee bairn, and look at her now, brazen as ye like, all she's after is the property.'

It took every ounce of Holly's self control not to turn round and speak her mind. But if she wanted to hear all they said she had to stand there and pretend not to listen. 'A bag of sugar, please, Mrs Muir.'

'Of course, if there hadn't been that pressure to get them oot.'

'And they'd nae one to defend them.'

'They just weren't strong enough to take it.'

'A pity their son was killed.'

'But the granddaughter. It was her duty. No conscience these youngsters.'

All these snippets reached Holly's ears and she grew hotter and more indignant by the second.

'I never dreamt they'd commit suicide, though. It just shows——'

Holly whirled, her heart thudding. She could keep silent no longer. 'Is that what you think?' she demanded, her green eyes sparking angrily, high colour flushing her cheeks. 'Is that why you're condemning me? It was only my grandfather who committed suicide, as you well know, the rest was an accident that no one could have foreseen.'

'So they say,' said the prim lady in glasses. 'That was the coroner's verdict. We happen to think differently.'

Holly looked from one pair of accusing eyes to another. 'Mr McEwen wouldn't lie, not to me, not to their own grandchild. He would tell me the truth. You're wrong, all of you, it's pure speculation.'

'The laird wouldn't want a scandal on his hands,' said Mrs Muir. 'It would be in his own interests to go along with the coroner's verdict.'

Holly pressed her fingers to her temples, feeling as though a heavy weight was closing in on her head. It was like a bad dream, all these distorted staring faces leering, censuring. 'I won't believe you. It can't be true. They wouldn't do a thing like that. They wouldn't have any reason.'

'When you're afraid of being evicted from your home,' said one of the old ladies, 'it's reason enough. You wouldn't know, you're too young, but you cannot adapt when you're old. All they wanted was to be left in peace.'

Holly went suddenly cold from the tip of her toes to the top of her head. She could feel her scalp stretching tightly, goose pimples raising themselves all over her body.

The room swam in a mist of rage such as she had never experienced before. Calum was responsible! Calum had wanted them out, the same as he wanted her out now. Whether he had done the vile deed himself, or whether he had used his mealy-mouthed henchman, it amounted to the same thing.

But there was one last question she wanted to ask before she went after him. 'Is it true, then, that my grandfather lost the cottage to James McEwen over a game of poker?'

'So the story goes,' said Mrs Muir. 'I'm sorry, lass, if this has all been a shock, but it doesnae change the way we feel. Your grandparents were a grand couple, always ready to help. It's a crying shame there was no one to help them.'

Holly could not stop the tears that rolled down her cheeks and as she paid for her provisions she was planning in her mind what she must do. Somehow Calum must be revenged for this terrible thing he had done. He was a murderer—and as such must be brought to justice.

CHAPTER NINE

HOLLY was hardly aware of driving back to Braeside. She had never in all her life felt so embittered, so disillusioned, so intensely angry.

She recalled the occasion when Calum had told her about the accident with the gun. She had been devastated—and he had been so gentle, and caring! God, what a fool she had been. She had swallowed his story hook, line and sinker—and all the time he knew that their deaths had been his fault. He had deliberately and purposefully blinded her with his own sensuality, and she, raving lunatic that she was, had fallen into his trap.

He must have known that once he got her on his side she would not believe any stories she might hear. Perhaps, if it had not been for that incident yesterday, if Duncan Gillies had not called and tried to kick her out, she would have attached no more importance to the story than any idle gossip usually tossed around in places as small as Invercray.

Now she knew better. The blinkers had fallen from her eyes and she could see him clearly for the man he was. He did not care about people. All that concerned him was that his estate ran smoothly. The fact that her grandfather had given his family loyal service for the whole of his working life did not enter into it. Calum had wanted him out. The result of this inhumanity did not bear thinking about.

As she put her groceries away Holly could feel the

unhappiness that had dogged the last few months of her grandparents' lives. Why, oh why, hadn't they written and explained? She would have been up like a shot and soon sorted Calum McEwen out.

The onus of guilt sat heavily on her shoulders. She should not have needed to be sent for. She ought to have come to see them. They had been her responsibility.

Strangely she did not blame her mother, even though her parent could equally be accused of neglecting them. Her mother had never made any pretence about liking her in-laws. Even now she would probably shrug and say it was a pity, but there was nothing at all she could have done about it.

She made herself a cup of strong coffee and debated what to do next. There was no point in going to Calum and accusing him outright. She had to be more devious than that. He was a clever man. The way she had been completely taken in proved it.

She could not eat, the thought of food choked her, and when it grew dark and she climbed the stairs to bed, she had still arrived at no decision.

From her window she looked up towards the forest of trees that surrounded Shilda House. She wondered if Calum knew exactly how much she hated and despised him. Her feelings ran so high that she would not be surprised if they were carried on the breeze and taken right up to him.

She gripped the windowsill so tightly that her fingers ached, but it was nothing compared to the ache in her heart. She felt as though it had been replaced by a brick, it hung so heavy.

Not surprisingly she slept little that night and when she got up it was to discover that the fine weather had changed. A mist rolled down from the hills and the surface of the loch was grey, whipped into tiny white waves by a north-easterly wind.

It matched her mood completely and suddenly she knew what she must do. Her first priority was to prove that the cottage was hers. No matter what everyone said she knew her grandfather would have changed his will if it truly no longer belonged to him.

Armed with this she would tackle Calum McEwen, or, better still, get the solicitor to do the job for her. She would go into Glasgow this morning and explain the situation. She really ought to have taken Steve's advice and done this before. He would have the power to dig out any information that was being withheld. Once that was done he could advise her regarding the possibility of prosecuting Calum for harassing her grandparents to such an extent that they had taken their own lives.

Of course, there might be nothing she could do. She did not know the way the law worked. Since the coroner had already made his decision that could be the end of it. In that case she would have to take matters into her own hands. For the time being, though, she would see what Mr Fraser could do.

The solicitor was as surprised as she had been to hear that the laird was claiming the cottage belonged to him.

'Your grandfather still held the deeds,' he said. 'In fact I have them in my possession. Unless Mr McEwen can provide written proof then I'm afraid there is nothing that he can do. The cottage is yours. A gentleman's agreement is simply not enough, especially since neither of the parties concerned are still living.'

Holly felt immediately better and left the building after Mr Fraser had promised he would be in touch with her once he had had a discussion with the laird. In fact she went into Glasgow and treated herself to a new dress to celebrate.

It was early evening when she finally returned to Braeside. The mist had lifted and the sky was a pale summer blue strung with feather-light clouds. A breeze still stirred the surface of the loch—and high up the mountain stood Shilda.

She stood and looked in its direction for several minutes, her breathing becoming deeper as her hatred of its owner burgeoned inside her. She was impatient to see him destroyed and hoped Mr Fraser would not take too long in proving the ownership.

When she discovered that the door of the cottage was ajar her heart stopped, then began again at double-quick time. It could be only one of two people who was in there—or who had been in there! She was almost afraid to go in for fear of what she might find.

She pushed the door open gingerly so as not to alert whoever might or might not be waiting, and tiptoed inside. There was no one in the tiny sitting room and everything seemed to be in order. She had half-expected to find it empty, to discover that the detestable Gillies had helped himself during her absence.

A faint sound in the kitchen led her in that direction. Her heart beat a tattoo so loudly it was like a drum in her ears, the blood raced through her veins, and her mouth felt as dry as a chamois.

If it was Duncan Gillies come to try again she would send him packing, threaten him with the law for breaking and entering. How had he opened the door? She had been so intent on catching the intruder that she had not looked to see whether the lock had been forced.

On the other hand it might be Calum. She hoped not. She was not ready for him yet. She wanted to be absolutely sure of her facts before confronting him, and she would need to be in full control of herself. It was no good facing him when she was half-afraid.

But the man she saw standing with his back to her was neither of these. 'Steve!' Her relief was enormous. What he was doing here she had no idea, but at least he would be on her side. He would be the ally she needed. One girl against two determined men was piling the odds a bit high.

Without stopping to observe that there was no smile of welcome she ran across the room and flung herself into his arms. 'Oh, Steve, thank goodness it's you. I need you so much.'

He held her for a moment then put her firmly from him. 'I can't really believe you mean that.' His face was stiff and white and he looked as though he had been going through some sort of trauma himself. 'You seem to be managing pretty well for yourself.'

'What do you mean?' she gasped. 'You've no idea what I've gone through this last twenty-four hours.'

'I think I have,' he said bitterly. 'I've been at Shilda House for most of the afternoon. I expected to find you there. Is there any particular reason why you keep dodging from one place to the other?'

'If you've seen Calum you'll know why,' she thrust angrily, picking up the kettle and filling it with water.

He moved out of her way as she set cups into saucers and filled the sugar basin and milk jug. She was tired and the last thing she wanted was another argument She had had enough of those to last a lifetime.

'I didn't see McEwen,' he said surprisingly, lighting a cigarette and inhaling deeply. 'He was out. But I did meet his—what do they call them up here?—his factor, Duncan Gillies. I expect you know him? We had a most enlightening talk.'

There was something in his expression that drained the colour from Holly's cheeks. Whatever Duncan had said it would not be to her credit, and whatever it was, it was clear Steve believed him. She could well imagine the lies that this man would tell to put her in the wrong, anything to get rid of her from this glen.

'Duncan Gillies is not a man to be trusted,' she said strongly. 'He's very good at doing other people's dirty work, and a little bit for himself into the bargain. He would stop at nothing to blacken anyone's character, and if you believe him you're an idiot.'

The kettle boiled and she warmed the pot, then spooned in tea and filled it with water. She set the cosy in position and all the time Steve looked at her as if she were something that had crawled out from under a stone.

When she could stand it no longer Holly cried, 'So, come on, let's have it. What lies has he been spreading? I'd like to know.'

Steve licked his lips and suddenly looked away. 'Is that tea ready? I think I'd like a cup first.'

'Are you sure you wouldn't like something stronger?' she cried angrily. 'I have some Scotch if it's your courage that needs bolstering. My God, Steve, anyone would think we were strangers instead of two people who——' She stopped. She had been about to say who were thinking of getting married. But perhaps that would be adding insult to injury judging by the mood he was in, so she finished lamely, 'have been friends for a long time.'

'I've discovered,' he said flatly, 'that I don't know you at all.' He poured his own tea and Holly was shocked to see that his hands trembled. 'I wish I'd never let you come here, on the other hand I might not have found out what sort of a girl you are until after we—were married.' He swallowed painfully and could not look her in the eye. 'So perhaps it was a good thing.'

'And what sort of person am I supposed to be?' she demanded, even though she could well imagine what stories Duncan had fabricated.

'You lied when you told me that there was nothing between you and McEwen,' he accused. 'Why, Holly? Why? I believed you, do you know that? I went home and called myself a fool for ever doubting you. I came back to apologise, to say that if this place meant so much to you I would pack up my job and we'd live here after we were married. That's how much you meant to me. And now——' he looked at her dully, 'I've discovered that you're no better than anyone else.'

'That's not true!' Holly was stung to defend herself. 'Whatever Duncan Gillies told you he's lying. It's his way of getting at me because he's trying to get me out of this cottage. He and Calum are in league with each other. I hate them both.'

Steve looked temporarily taken aback. 'In that case you'll have no hesitation in denying that you and McEwen——' He seemed to be having difficulty in finding suitable words, 'were seen—together—yesterday afternoon?'

The colour came back into Holly's cheeks with a vengeance and guilt was in her eyes before she could hide it. Duncan Gillies had been spying all right and he had used the information to his advantage—or so he thought. Steve would have told him who he was and Duncan would probably imagine that Steve would drag her away from here rather than let her indulge in an affair with Calum.

It proved how little he knew of human nature. It was the very worst thing he could have said so far as Steve was concerned. For herself, well, maybe he had done her a favour. She would have had to tell Steve she no longer felt deeply enough to want to marry him. Now there was no need. He would not want her now.

'You don't have to answer,' he said thickly, stubbing out his cigarette with quick angry movements. 'I can see by your face that it is true. You disappoint me, Holly, you really do. I thought you were above that sort of thing.'

She sighed and looked down at her hands. 'I'm sorry, Steve, except that it's not quite so bad as you think. I'm not trying to make excuses for myself, it's too late for that, but—we didn't go—all the way. I thought I loved him, and I thought he loved me, then I found out that it was just a physical thing with him. It's all over—not that it ever really began—but—well—I'd like you to know.'

It was Steve's turn to sigh and he looked uncomfortable as he finished his tea and put the cup on the table. 'Thanks for telling me,' he said. 'I didn't really want to believe Gillies, but he sounded so sincere. What are you going to do?'

'I'm staying here,' she said firmly. 'There's rather more at stake now than I first thought. Calum told me that my grandparents died in a shooting accident, but I've heard a rumour that it was suicide—and I intend finding out.'

Steve looked shocked and lit another cigarette. 'Hell, Holly, that's bit rough. What on earth made them do a thing like that?'

She compressed her lips. 'Pressure to get out of the cottage, would you believe? And I don't need to have it spelt out to know who's behind that. I had some of the same treatment myself. But he's not dealing with a couple of old people who were not sure of their rights now. He has me to contend with. I've done what you said and put the matter into the hands of the solicitor. That's where I've been today. I can't wait to see what he comes up with.'

'Do you want me to stay?' asked Steve.

'No.' Holly shook her head. 'You'd lose your job and there's no point in that. I can cope, don't worry.'

He smiled wryly. 'I always knew you were one hell of a tough character. perhaps we were never really matched. you sometimes make me feel quite—inferior. Mandy says that——' He stopped and looked embarrassed.

'You've been seeing Mandy again?' Holly suddenly did not feel so bad about letting him down. 'I'm glad, she's sweet, you'll be able to look after her. She'll never go off and do her own thing, you can be sure of that.'

She saw now why he had come. He had wanted to make sure which of them he really wanted. Of one thing she was certain, he had never expected to find anything like this. He looked devastated, poor man.

'Are you hungry?' she asked. 'Do you fancy an omelette and chips?'

'I'd really rather get back,' he said. 'I have to be at work in the morning.'

'Where's your car?' frowned Holly.

He smiled ruefully. 'Up at Shilda House. I left it there and walked down with Duncan.'

'And how did you get in here?'

'He had a key. Do you think that wise, Holly, especially under the circumstances?'

'Damn!' she exploded and bounced from the room. A swift glance soon disclosed that the lock had been changed yet again. She would not have been able to get in unless she had broken yet another window. He had begun his campaign already!

'I think you ought to come back with me,' said Steve worriedly, 'and let your solicitor sort everything out. It's obvious both McEwen and Gillies have got it in for you. Who knows what they'll come up with next.'

Holly's chin jutted more firmly than ever and her eyes glinted like jade set in ice. 'I owe it to my grandparents to stick this out. If I go now Calum will have won.'

'I can't see that it's really so important,' argued Steve, pushing a hand worriedly through his crop of sandy hair. 'Mr Fraser will ensure that justice is done. Can't you leave it to him?'

'That's what you would do, isn't it, Steve?' Holly looked at him sadly. 'But I'm not you. I'm a fighter. No one puts on me and gets away with it. Mr Fraser can help, I know that, but I intend to be around while the battle is going on.'

He sighed heavily. 'And there's nothing I can say that will make you change your mind?'

Holly shook her head. This had become a personal

vendetta between herself and Calum, with Duncan Gillies thrown in to stack the odds against her. She actually felt quite excited at the thought of bringing the great laird to his knees. He had humiliated her by believing that all she was after was a physical relationship. Now it was her turn to humiliate him.

'I'll drive you up to the house,' she said. 'It will save you a bit of time if you're really intent on getting back tonight. Once you hit the motorway it won't take long.'

'You aren't going to leave the house unlocked?'

She laughed. 'This isn't Walsall. No one ever really bothers to lock up around here.'

'Except when there are cads like McEwen about,' he said darkly.

'If he wants to get in he will whether it's locked or not,' said Holly patiently. 'I'm not scared of him or Gillies. In fact it would give me a lot of pleasure to use my judo training on either one of them.' No need to tell Steve that Calum was an expert in the art too. 'But—if it will make you happy I'll take the back door key. It's a bit big to carry around but——' She stopped short as she suddenly noticed that an extra lock had been fitted. As well as the ancient one with the heavy key there was a Yale lock. It was bright and shiny, leering insolently, and she could not think why she had not spotted it before.

'He's very determined,' said Steve unhappily.

'So am I,' said Holly with a sweet smile. 'I think I'm going to enjoy this. Come on, let's go, let's leave all the doors wide. Who cares? I can always break another window if they come and close them in my absence.'

Holly felt quite reckless as she drove Steve up to

Shilda House. She was filled with a heady excitement, as though she was drunk, a couldn't-care-less attitude that baffled Steve and pleased herself.

It proved that what she had thought was love was nothing more than the same physical attraction Calum had felt for her. Now she could meet him on an equal footing. In fact his desire to get rid of her was matched by her determination to stay.

Holly was not consciously aware that she hoped for a confrontation with Calum, but felt extraordinarily disappointed when he was nowhere in sight. Steve's car was on the cobbled courtyard where he had left it and no one came out to check who was taking it away.

It was with reluctance that he said goodbye. 'Promise me,' he said, 'that you'll do nothing stupid. If things get nasty come home, please. I'd like to think that we're still friends.'

She kissed him gently on the cheek. 'Of course, Steve, we'll always be that, and I shall come back anyway once I've achieved my object. There's nothing for me here now that Calum's made his feelings plain. Give Mandy my regards—and I hope she'll make you happier than I have. Oh, and how's my dear mother? I haven't heard a word from her.'

He shrugged. 'I passed on your message. But you know what she thinks of Scotland. She said she'd write but how long that will take is anyone's guess.'

Holly accepted this philosophically. It was no more and no less than she was used to. For a long time now there had been no love lost between herself and her mother. Her parent would write, when she was good and ready, and not a day before.

When she arrived back at Braeside some of her buoyancy faded. It was dark now, the sky spangled with myriad stars, a half-moon reflected in the still waters of the loch.

She stood for a moment and drank in the sweet fragrance of the night, the roses round the door, the honeysuckle over an old tree-stump. From the forest came the occasional cu-ic of a nightjar, the drawn-out hoot of a long-eared owl.

Eventually she went inside and closing the door leaned back against it, not bothering for a moment to put on the light. It was a second or two before she became aware that there was someone else in the room. It was a sensation more than anything else. She could not see nor hear anyone, but the hairs prickled on the back of her neck as she reached out and snapped the switch.

Calum sat on her grandfather's chair, his powerful legs stretched out lazily, his long-fingered hands resting on the arms. Apart from blinking a couple of times when the room was flooded with light he appeared remarkably relaxed, smiling even as he looked across at her.

To Holly's intense annoyance her heart began a crazy tattoo. Maybe her mind knew that she no longer wanted anything more to do with him, but her heart certainly did not. It responded like metal to a magnet. She felt as drawn to him as if they had never had words.

But none of this showed on her face. She folded her arms and shot sparks from her eyes. 'What do you want?'

'Now there's a greeting,' he said, pretending to look hurt.

Holly tossed her auburn curls. 'Why should I welcome a man who's doing everything in his power to kick me out of this house? What do you want, McEwen?'

There was a fractional hardening in those dark eyes at the harshness of her tone, a cruel tightening of his lips, and knuckles gleamed white as he pushed himself up.

Holly had forgotten quite how tall he was. She decided she preferred him sitting. At least then he did not fill the room. Again he gave that suffocating impression of taking over the place and she felt herself gasping for air.

'I want to know why you have not turned up at the office for two days.'

Her mouth fell open at the unexpectedness of the question. 'Isn't it obvious? My God, you surely don't expect me to work for you after—what you did?'

His chin firmed and he stared at her coldly. 'As I recall you were quite a willing party to everything that happened. But I haven't come here to discuss that. The way I see it one's private life should never interfere with one's business life. You are still employed by me and therefore I shall expect you to be at the office at nine sharp in the morning.'

'Go to hell!' said Holly rudely.

'How unladylike,' returned Calum, 'but it matters not. I have work that needs doing and you are the one who is going to do it.'

'Am I?' cried Holly. 'How do you propose making me?' It was like fixing herself on to the end of a bayonet, looking into his eyes. They pierced her thoroughly and painfully and the pit of her stomach curled into a tight knot as she held herself rigidly against the door. But she must not back down. This man was her adversary. He was the enemy in the camp. There must be only one winner, and that was herself.

'If necessary I shall take you by force.' There was a gleam to his eyes that was different to any expression she had seen before. 'Once there I don't think you'll be difficult.'

'I expect you're wishing you had never changed your mind about Miss Drummond?' Holly threw the taunt across the room.

But it was adeptly caught and tossed back. 'Miss Drummond would have been as irksome as toothache. I like your company, Holly. I find it stimulating.'

'Because we're always crossing swords?'

He smiled slowly. 'Not always, my little friend.'

It was not difficult to guess what he was thinking and to her dismay Holly felt her cheeks grow warm. 'From now on we will be,' she said. 'I don't know why you're trying to be nice to me after you've gone to the trouble of changing the locks again. I think you're despicable.'

His head jerked. 'I've touched no locks.'

'Maybe *you* haven't,' she returned sarcastically, 'but your disciple has.'

'Duncan? Why should he do that?'

Holly had not realised he was such a good actor. He looked genuinely puzzled. 'Don't try that on,' she spat. 'We both know you're in collusion. He wants me out because you do.'

'Nonsense,' said Calum strongly. 'This is a personal issue, as you well know. It has nothing at all to do with Duncan.'

Holly glared. 'Are you denying that you sent him down here yesterday to get rid of me?'

'I most certainly am.' He stepped towards her, a frown darkening his brow.

Holly felt a throb of response and cursed her traitorous heart. She edged round the room away from him, and then to her total embarrassment her stomach rumbled loudly.

Calum looked at her sharply. 'When did you last eat?'

She shrugged. 'Breakfast, I think.'

He cursed. 'You fool. Sit down and I'll fix you something. You have stocked your pantry, I suppose?'

And although the last thing Holly wanted was for him to use her kitchen she obeyed. She did feel strangely weak, though the was not so sure it was lack of food so much as Calum's presence.

It was odd how he still affected her despite the animosity she felt over the way he had treated her grandparents. It was as if her hate and love went hand in hand, and it was difficult to differentiate between the two.

She gave up trying to work it out and closed her eyes, listening with half of her mind to the sounds of Calum working in the kitchen, wondering how long it would be before Fraser had any news for her.

One thing was sure, once Calum had a letter from the solicitor he would realise how much in earnest she was. He could deny as much as he liked the fact that he was still trying to get her out. She knew it was true and was determined to stay put until it was proved conclusively who the real owner was.

She was almost asleep when he told her it was ready. He had cooked enough for the two of them and as they chewed their way through bacon and mushrooms, sausage and tomatoes, as well as slices of crisply fried bread, Holly found herself forgetting they were supposed to be enemies.

'I didn't know you could cook,' she said, when she finally put down her knife and fork and poured them both a second cup of tea.

'Any man worth his salt can do a fry-up,' he grinned. 'It's about all I am good at, and I've no doubt Hamilton would have a fit if he saw how I throw everything into the pan. What did Steve want?'

He had a way of flooring her with unexpected questions. She stared for a moment before answering, not at all sure whether it would be advisable to tell him that it was all over between them. In the end she decided against it. Steve was her protection.

'Isn't it natural for a man who's asked a girl to marry him to want to come and see her?'

'I thought you had fallen out?'

She could not quite meet his eyes. 'Steve is not the sort to hold it against me simply because I would not go back with him. He understands how much this cottage means to me.'

'I wonder if he knows how much he means to you.'

Holly jerked her head up quickly. 'And what is that supposed to mean?'

'I don't think I need spell it out,' he said softly. 'If you really loved Steve you would never have let me anywhere near you.'

Holly's hand fluttered to her throat. 'That doesn't necessarily follow. Just because I feel a physical attraction for you it doesn't mean I don't love Steve. We have a perfect relationship.'

His eyes fixed on the nervous movements of her fingers and he gave her a peculiar tight-lipped smile. 'Can he satisfy you sexually?'

He knew, thought Holly, that there was no man on earth who could fulfil her like he could. 'Why the inquest?' she snapped, running the tip of her tongue over suddenly dry lips.

'Because I don't want to see you ruin your life.' There was a hungry look in his eyes which she found totally hypnotising.

Her heart began to beat so loud it drowned all other sounds in the room and she had the strangest feeling that something momentous was going to happen. 'Why?' she whispered. 'What does it matter to you?'

Instead of answering he stood up and walked round to her side of the table. He took her hands and pulled her to her feet and although Holly knew she ought to resist, she discovered she had not the slightest desire to do so.

Instead she stood still and silent and waited for him to speak. 'It shouldn't matter at all,' he muttered thickly, 'but, hell, Holly, I don't want you to marry Steve.' His face twisted in agony. 'I want you to marry me.'

CHAPTER TEN

HOLLY wondered whether she had heard Calum correctly. It was the last thing she had expected him to say. 'Why?' she managed to husk at last, all the time her mind trying to work out for itself the answer to her question. Her green eyes had never been wider, nor so beautiful. Her lips trembled as she puzzled over what he had said.

'Why does a man usually ask a woman to marry him?' he asked softly, gripping her hands more tightly, an intensity on his face that she found difficult to accept. He looked deeply moved, yet how could he be?

Love was the last reason he could have for asking her. She recalled the occasion he told her he had no intention of getting married. 'Heaven forbid!' he had said strongly. 'I want no woman trying to change my way of life.' He had meant it then and she was quite sure he was not the sort of person to change his mind.

It was to prevent her from digging too deeply into the true reason behind her grandparents' sudden death, that was it. He did not wish her to see him in a bad light. This was a feeble excuse, but the only one she could come up with, and she made herself believe it.

She worked herself up into a fury, seeing him as selfish and mean, interested only in himself. With a cry she wrenched herself free. 'Not for the reasons you have in mind,' she cried. 'I hate you and I wouldn't marry you if you offered me a million pounds.'

Calum looked disturbed by her outburst. 'I've shocked you, Holly,' he said at once. 'I'm sorry, I shouldn't have sprung it on you so quickly, but I can't bear the thought of you marrying that bore.'

'That doesn't mean you have to ask me to marry you,' she cried savagely. 'Only the day before yesterday you told me you did not love me, and I'm not so stupid as to think you've had a change of heart. I know why you're asking me, but you might as well save your breath. I'm going to follow this thing right through and there's nothing you can do to stop me.'

'My God!' exclaimed Calum. 'I'm not doing it to get you to withdraw your complaint to Fraser. I have no fear of his probing. I can only tell him what I told you. There's no written proof, not that I know of. I only have my father's word, but I'm certainly not trying to swindle you. Hell, Holly, why should I do that?'

She eyed him heatedly. 'I'm not talking about this place. I've discovered something about you that's far worse and far more important.' Her small high breasts rose and fell as her breathing grew ragged, and she clenched her fists so tightly that her nails dug painfully into her palms.

Calum's eyes shot wide and he seemed to stiffen, as though he had a very good idea what she was going to say, but when he spoke there was nothing in his voice to indicate that he was troubled. In fact he sounded remarkably composed. He even smiled. 'I can't think of anything I've done that's so awful.'

'I don't expect you to admit it,' she hissed through gritted teeth. 'But I have no doubt it is true.'

'Then suppose you tell me what this terrible thing is?' There was a stillness about him that at one time would have terrified her. Now it merely served to increase her anger.

'Your version of how my grandparents died,' she shrilled. 'It was lies, all lies, but I was so gullible that I believed you. I even let you console me.' Her lip curled. 'You must have been laughing at that one.'

Calum's thick brows beetled into a straight line above his handsome black eyes, and he drew himself up so that he appeared even taller and broader than before. 'It was true, Holly.' His lips were grim as he watched her closely.

He thinks I'm bluffing, she thought. He wonders what I'm going to say next. 'I prefer to believe it was suicide,' she said acidly, watching for his reaction, not disappointed when she saw a flicker of shock cross those dark eyes.

'Who's told you that?' The clipped question shot like a bullet from a gun.

'Does it matter?' Never had she felt so enraged. The blood pounded through her head, her vision blurred. She saw Calum through a haze of red mist, and the fact that he was so calm and detached added fuel to her anger. 'I know, that's sufficient, and I also know why they did it.'

'Holly, *Holly!*' He tried to take her into his arms. 'You've been listening to gossip.'

She swung away and regarded him coldly. 'Gossip or not I happen to believe it.'

'My dear, it's all lies. Please, Holly, don't destroy yourself like this.' Again he attempted to touch her and again Holly lurched away.

'I might have known you'd try to get out of it, but it's too late, I've already asked Mr Fraser to do whatever is necessary.'

His brows creased and he looked bewildered. 'You're blaming me?'

Holly felt so keyed up that she knew it would only be a few minutes before she lost control. 'Don't act the innocent, for goodness' sake,' she screamed. 'If you hadn't thrown your weight around they would still be alive.'

He drew in a deep rasping breath. 'Are you suggesting that in some way I caused their death?'

'I am saying,' she said icily, 'that you killed them.'

His jaw firmed as he pulled his lips together in a grim line. 'Libel, Holly, is a very serious offence. May I ask on what foundation you are basing this statement?' There was nothing now on his face to indicate that only minutes earlier he had asked her to marry him. It was hard and totally uncompromising.

She took a couple of deep breaths before answering. 'You wanted them out of this cottage. You made their lives hell. What chance had they to defend themselves?'

He tried to interrupt but she went on, 'They had no one to help them fight, Calum. They wanted to end their days here in this house where they had spent their lives together. They did not want to leave and find somewhere new. You gave them no alternative.'

'Holly, please——'

But she would not listen. 'Don't try to get out of it. Whether you or your despicable henchman did the dirty work it makes no difference. He was acting on your orders. Don't forget I've had a taste of what he's like. Second to you he's the most obnoxious character I've ever met!'

She stopped to draw breath and Calum took the opportunity to grab her shoulders and shake her as one might a rag doll. 'You're out of your mind, Holly. I liked the Burns. I wouldn't have dreamt of making their lives a misery.'

She glared fiercely and everything around her faded. All she could see was the hypnotic blackness of his eyes, steady and unblinking, willing her to believe him.

She could hear his heart as well as her own. She could feel the heat of his body and the blood pounding in her ears. And she was afraid she would weaken.

With strength born of desperation she pushed him away and flew across the room. 'Get out!' she shrieked. 'Get out, you murderer. The next time I want to see you is in court.'

For several minutes Calum stood and looked at her. His face was drawn and pale, a muscle jerked in his jaw, and there was a bleakness in his eyes that chilled Holly's heart.

This was the absolute end, she thought. There was no going back now. She had made her feelings clear, even if it did mean losing the opportunity to marry the one man she truly loved. It was better this way, there could be no lasting happiness with a man who had been instrumental in her grandparents' deaths, she would for ever hold it against him—and ultimately it would destroy their relationship.

'Is that your last word?' There was a peculiar strangled sound to his voice, revealing that he was in the grip of an emotion which he was trying his hardest to subdue.

She nodded, her throat hurting as she fought back a sudden desire to cry. She must not weaken. Calum must never know how much it was costing to send him away.

'You're making a grave mistake,' he muttered thickly. 'You'll get nowhere.'

'If I don't, it won't be for the want of trying.' She flung him a contemptuous smile and turned away. When she next looked he had gone.

She sat down and forced herself to take several deep breaths. She refused to cry. She had done what had to be done. It was the only solution.

After ten minutes of controlled breathing she began to relax. Her jaw ached because she had clenched her teeth so hard, and there were imprints in her palms where she had dug her nails in, but she felt better. Her vendetta was still on and one way or another she was going to win.

She knew she would have difficulty in sleeping so she poured and drank a glass of her grandfather's malt whisky, taking another glass up to bed with her. Unused as she was to alcohol her head spun crazily, but it did the trick and minutes later she was asleep.

Dawn heralded another of those grey misty mornings when the top of the mountain was lost and the loch looked grey and uninviting. It mirrored her mood exactly. She had a headache, caused no doubt by the whisky, and felt thoroughly out of tune with the world.

She ate a slice of toast and drank several cups of strong tea, and decided to go for a walk to clear her head. To protect herself from the moist damp air she pulled on a bright orange cagoule, but before she had even opened the door someone knocked on it. She had heard no vehicle and the sound startled her, making her run to the window and peer out.

Her spirits dipped even lower when she saw the kilted figure of Calum's factor, and she toyed with the idea of pretending to be out. She had no wish for a confrontation with him, not after her set-to with

Calum yesterday. She still felt too fragile. On the other hand he would not hesitate to enter if he thought the cottage empty.

With reluctance she opened the door, glaring hostilely into the thin pinched face. 'Yes?' she said loudly, making it very clear that he was not welcome.

'So you're still here!' His almost invisible brows lifted, deepening the lines that grooved his high forehead.

Holly found the splodgy pale eyes more repulsive than ever and had difficulty in repressing a shudder. 'Naturally. It would take more of a man than you to frighten me away.'

He stiffened and before she could stop him shouldered his way inside. 'You're a foolish young lassie,' he said tersely. 'You're the one who's going to get hurt.'

She slammed the door and eyed him coldly. 'Don't think I'd be afraid to fetch the police. You've already broken the law by changing the locks on property that does not belong to you—I know Calum McEwen told you to do it, but that doesn't make the slightest difference. This cottage is mine, do you hear? And it's staying mine, and I'd thank you to leave—right now.'

He took no notice, sitting down in one of the comfortable armchairs as though he owned the place. 'I'm disappointed in your boyfriend. I really thought he would persuade you to leave. He told me he had no intention of going back without you.'

'And of course you encouraged him? You no doubt told him that I was fighting a losing battle. You don't know me, Mr Gillies. When I dig my heels in no one, but no one, gets rid of me.'

'And I'm afraid you don't know me, Miss Burns. I

don't take kindly to having my carefully laid plans shot to pieces in front of my eyes—especially by a bit of a thing like you.'

It was amazing, thought Holly, how eyes so pale could burn so fiercely. His hatred was electrifying. But he was talking in riddles. 'What plans?' she asked crisply. 'Are you after this cottage for yourself? Is that why you're trying to get me out?'

He shook his head scornfully. 'What would I want with a wee place like this? It's Isabel I'm concerned about.'

Holly frowned. 'And who, might I ask, is Isabel?'

'Isabel Drummond.' He sounded impatient, as though she ought to know very well who the woman was.

'Ah!' she said. 'The secretary lady. I didn't realise you knew her. Is Calum thinking of setting her on again since I've—er, withdrawn my services?'

'I think he should,' said the thin man sharply.

'And you have some say in his affairs?' Holly could not accept that this little man did the hiring of Calum's staff. Farmhands, yes, but surely not girls to do his office work?

'Isabel is eminently suitable. She is fully trained, is smart, and only a few years younger than the laird himself. She is in every way the perfect person for the job.'

His enthusiasm surprised Holly. 'In that case why hasn't he employed her before?'

The factor looked at her condemningly. 'The laird usually does his own choosing—with disastrous results.'

She knew what he meant, it was there in his eyes, and she shook her head angrily. 'So you think he ought to rely on your judgment? I can't see him taking too kindly to that.'

The factor's chin jutted. 'If he gave her a chance he would see how right I am.'

He was a determined old man, she would give him that. There was something fanatical about him, as though a great deal more hinged on Miss Drummond getting this job than he was admitting.

'I'm sure you'll be able to convince him,' she said drily. 'But if she's really such a find then I'm also sure he won't object to her living at the house. There's no need to get me out of this cottage.'

He sniffed, his pinched nose growing thinner and sharper. 'He won't have her there. He's having no more secretaries there, so he said.' He looked at her accusingly, and she knew he was wondering how she had managed it herself.

'Then she can always stay with you,' said Holly sweetly.

The nervous tic that she had spotted once before suddenly began to work in his face. 'That wouldn't do,' he said quickly, almost feverishly. 'That wouldn't do at all.'

'Why?' she asked bluntly.

For the first time he looked unsure of himself. 'There isn't room,' he blundered, 'besides, it's too far away.'

He was hiding something and Holly wanted to know what. 'What is she to you?' she asked sharply.

'Why should she be anything?' he prevaricated, crossing and recrossing his thin legs.

'It's something you don't want Calum to find out, isn't it?' Holly was determined not to give up. 'You needn't worry, your secret will be safe with me. I've finished with the laird, *for ever*.'

'You have?' he asked eagerly. 'Is it all over?'

She nodded, then gasped as a sudden thought struck her. 'You're not hoping that Isabel Drummond and Calum will—make a go of it?' She swallowed convulsively. 'Surely you're not matchmaking?' There might be no chance of her marrying Calum herself, but it sure as hell hurt to think of him with someone else.

His nod was barely perceptible, and in seconds he changed from a tough aggressive character to a simpering little man. 'It's my granddaughter, you see. I want to help her. She's thirty-one and not married—and well, it doesn't seem likely she'll get many offers now. The laird would be perfect. She'd have the life of a lady, all the money she could spend, and——'

'Has she two heads or something?' interrupted Holly cuttingly. 'If no one else wants her what makes you so sure Calum McEwen will be any different? I'm sure his taste in women runs much higher than your granddaughter.' If she was anything like this weedy little man Calum would never look twice at her. Maybe that was why he had wanted to house her in this cottage.

Duncan's head jerked and the fire returned to his eyes. 'I didn't ask for your insolence. Isabel is a grand girl. She's an excellent secretary, a good cook and housekeeper, and would make the laird a very good wife.'

'He doesn't need a cook or a housekeeper,' said Holly coolly. 'But he does need a damn good lover. What's your granddaughter like in bed? Would she be able to satisfy him?'

Her outrageous comments shocked him, as she had known they would, and he pushed himself jerkily to his feet, his normally pallid face suffused with colour. 'Have ye no sense of decency, Miss Burns? Or is it no more than I can expect from your generation? Thank goodness my Isabel is not like you. She is a decent Christian lassie.'

And so prim and virtuous that no one wants her, thought Holly disrespectfully, feeling an illogical hatred for this unknown woman. 'Does Calum know she is your granddaughter?'

Duncan Gillies shook his head. 'The laird would think I was after a favour and that's not what I want at all. It is a chance for Isabel.'

'Then you'll have to think of somewhere else for her to live,' said Holly, 'because I'm staying put. If you harass me any further I shall call in the police. Something my grandparents should have done. I wish they had let me know what was going on, I'd have been up here in a flash. There's only so much people can take, you know.'

He looked suddenly alarmed, but said roughly. 'I haven't the slightest idea what you are talking about.'

'Oh, come on,' she said. 'You know as well as I do that you and Calum made their lives a misery trying to get them out.'

The factor eyed her apprehensively and moved hurriedly towards the door. 'I don't know where you've heard that story, but it's a load of lies, all of it.'

'In that case,' she returned smoothly, 'I'm sure it won't disturb you to hear that I've put the matter in the hands of my solicitor. I would imagine that both you and Calum will have to stand trial.'

Her bluff succeeded because he shot through the door like a hunted rabbit, glancing only once over his shoulder, revealing a face that had lost its bravado. So much for the tough act, she thought, smiling wryly to herself.

She did not really think that Duncan had done anything more than carry out orders, but if her threat had done nothing else it had at least succeeded in getting him off her back. She felt sure he would not trouble her again.

Once the Land Rover was out of sight she set off on her walk. She took the path around the loch but the moisture-loaded mist closed in all about her, soaking her jeans and shoes, settling in her hair like clusters of diamonds. Instead of being pretty and inviting everywhere was cold and grey and she decided it had been a mistake to come out.

She hurried back and lit a fire to dry her wet clothes and in a sudden burst of activity decided to give the cottage a thorough clean. She started upstairs and worked her way down, polishing windows and furniture, hoovering up every speck of dust and dirt, and thoroughly enjoying herself into the bargain.

In the sitting room near the door was an old dresser which she imagined had never been moved since it had been put there. It was time, she resolved, to chase out the spiders. It took all her strength to drag it forward and she found all sorts of bits and pieces that had fallen behind.

Recipes cut out of magazines, coupons offering money off margarine and tea, used envelopes, even a notebook with a whole year's household expenses. Her grandfather would certainly have wondered where that had got to. And an envelope still sealed!

She remembered it was their custom to drop the post down on top of the dresser and it was easy to see how this one had slipped down the back.

Whoever had written, though, would never have received a reply.

It was not until she was about to slit the envelope that she realised it was not addressed to her grandparents after all but Mr Fraser in Glasgow. Her grandfather obviously thought he had posted it, and how long it had lain there was anyone's guess. It was very yellow as though it had been lost for years.

Holly debated whether to forward the envelope with an explanatory note, or open it for herself. It could well be that the communication had no relevance after all this time.

Curiosity got the better of her and with her heart beating at twice its normal rate she opened the envelope. A cursory glance was enough for her to see that it was a will, and a letter in her grandfather's hand explaining why the need for a new one had arisen. Braeside was no longer his. He had lost it fairly and squarely to James McEwen over a game of poker. He even mentioned that he was sorry it would not now go to his granddaughter, but at least she would never know what she had missed. The letter was dated twelve years ago.

It would be about that time, she thought, when she had heard her grandfather arguing with the old laird. This must have been what it was all about.

By the time she had finished reading her fingers were shaking and she sat down with the papers on her lap. Naturally she would have to take it to Mr Fraser, but it meant that Calum had been right and she was wrong, and, tough as it sounded, he had been perfectly within his rights to evict her grandparents from this cottage.

She thought about it for a long time and because she

was basically honest decided she owed him an apology. But she could not face him. That was too much. She would write him a letter and drop it in at Shilda House when she left the glen.

She could not stay, not now, not now that she knew it was no longer hers. She looked around at the familiar furnishings and felt sad. She would miss it. In the few days she had been here it had felt more like home than the house in Walsall ever had. It was ridiculous, but she felt as though she belonged here, and it was going to be a hard wrench to tear herself away.

Eventually she pushed back the dresser and finished tidying the room. Her jeans had dried so she folded them and put them in her case. She packed all her other things too, adding a photograph of her grandparents but deciding that to take anything else would be too painful.

It was rather late to begin the journey home today so she made herself an early supper and went to bed. The next morning the mist had cleared and it was another of those bright summer days that turned the glen into a magical place.

She loaded all her stuff into the car and after one last remorseful look at the cottage drove up to Shilda House. She knew Calum's routine well enough to know that he would be out—otherwise she would not have dared make this journey.

Her letter to him was brief. She mentioned her discovery of an amended will and a letter revealing that Alasdair Burns was no longer the owner of Braeside. She apologised for doubting his word and enclosed the keys to the cottage. 'It's all yours,' she finished. 'I'm going back to Walsall today. I expect you'll be relieved never to see me again.'

As she pushed the envelope beneath the heavy oak door with the grinning fox's head it swung open. Calum, in a thin black sweater and jodhpurs, with the inevitable black boots, looked down at her.

He did not look as surprised to see her as she was him and she wondered whether he had watched her arrival. His face was devoid of all expression as he bent to retrieve the envelope. Holly stood in silence as he ripped it open and read the contents. She would have given anything to avoid this last confrontation. Anything!

He looked exactly the same as he had on that first meeting, and she knew that for as long as she lived she would never forget him. Even now her body responded in a way that made her feel ashamed. He was the only man who could do this to her, who could make her want him even though she knew it was a futile emotion.

When he had finished reading he looked at her and those dark eyes had never been more powerful. She felt herself slowly disintegrating. There was nothing on his face to suggest that the news was welcome and she wished she had not come. She wished she had posted the letter instead.

'I was just on my way down to see you,' he said at length. 'Perhaps you'd like to come inside. There's something I want to say.'

Holly hesitated, quite sure there was nothing at all that wouldn't be best left unsaid. 'I'm leaving the glen,' she returned thinly, 'and since I've got to call in and see Mr Fraser first I'd really rather go now. I don't want to be late getting home.'

His lips firmed as if he found her excuse irksome. 'It won't take long, but it is important; to me, at least. You've made your apologies, I'd like to make mine.'

'For what?' she asked sharply, her eyes widening in surprise. Calum apologising was as rare as finding a four-leaved clover.

'For Duncan Gillies' behaviour,' he said surprisingly. 'We've had quite an enlightening talk.' He stepped back into the hall and Holly entered because now she was curious to hear what this was all about.

They went into the panelled room where she had made that first phone call to Steve. There was no fire this morning but it still smelled of roses and wax polish and she felt instantly at ease. She had always liked this room, it had a nice atmosphere, and today was no exception.

She declined Calum's offer of a glass of whisky, standing patiently while he poured one for himself. She wanted to suggest that it was a little early in the morning to be drinking, but did not feel he would take kindly to such a statement.

When he stood looking out of the window while he sipped his drink she grew restless. 'I haven't got all day, Calum,' she said tightly. 'Would you mind getting on with it.'

He swung round and for a moment it did not look as though he knew where to begin. 'I believe my factor has been doing and saying quite a lot without my knowledge,' he said tensely. 'I'm not trying to excuse my behaviour towards you when you first arrived, I realise that it gave you every reason to distrust me, but believe me, Holly, it was never my intention that you should be threatened. Duncan overstepped the mark when he came to see you. He's a good man but inclined to be zealous. I want to reassure you that it will not happen again.'

'Is that all?' asked Holly coolly. 'You needn't have

bothered. I think I managed to persuade Mr Gillies that I was capable of looking after my own interests. As it happens you were right about the cottage, and I do apologise, but that does not mean that I forgive you for persecuting my grandparents. I know you were within your rights—but for them to have done what they did—well—you must have come down on them pretty hard. I don't think action like that was called for.'

'Again,' said Calum with remarkable patience, patience such as she had never seen him exercise before, 'that was Duncan, not me. Lord knows what the man was trying to prove, but believe me, I had no idea he was constantly on their backs.'

'And I'm supposed to accept that?' asked Holly bitterly.

He sighed deeply and his face looked strangely white and drawn. 'I'd like you to. I saw him leave the cottage yesterday morning so I stopped him and asked why he had come to see you. It all came out then. I don't know what you said to him but the man looked as frightened as hell.' He smiled wryly. 'I'd forgotten how tough you can get when you're riled. You sure set Duncan thinking.'

'Good,' she said tightly, but guessed she had not frightened Duncan enough for him to confess about his granddaughter. That was a dream he was still hoping would come true. 'It doesn't alter the fact, though, that my grandparents committed suicide.'

'Holly.' Calum set down his glass and came towards her. 'I'm quite sure that none of it was premeditated. Once before your grandfather accidentally fired his gun, fortunately no one was within range. I tried to persuade him then to give up hunting. He was far too old and forgetful for that sort of thing. But he would not listen.'

He put his hands on her shoulders and his eyes were full of pain as he looked into her face. 'You're very much like him, Holly. As stubborn as they come. Nothing, not even Duncan's harassment would have made him turn that gun on his wife deliberately. On himself, yes, after he had killed her. It would be too much for any man to live with.' He paused, and then continued gently, 'I was at the inquest, Holly. I testified that your grandfather was not as careful as he should be. There was no suggestion that he had deliberately taken their two lives because they could not face the thought of leaving the cottage.'

By the time he had finished Holly was leaning weakly against him. She had no reason to doubt that he was telling her the truth. He sounded as upset as she was herself.

He held her close and Holly knew she was in danger of giving away her true feelings. This was where she belonged, she did not want to go away, she ought to have accepted Calum's proposal, no matter that he did not love her. It would have been better than the lifetime of unhappiness she had committed herself to.

'Why did you ask me to marry you?' She did not realise she had spoken her thoughts out loud, and was appalled when Calum took her face between his big gentle hands and looked kindly down into her eyes.

'Because,' he said, 'I wanted to spend the rest of my life with you. Because you are beautiful. Because I did not want you to marry Steve. Oh, Holly, I can think of a thousand and one reasons why I want to marry you.'

'You still want to?' Her eyes had never been wider

nor more luminous. Her lips trembled as she looked up into the shining blackness of his.

'But of course,' he muttered brokenly, 'why else do you think I was coming to see you? I had to put things right between us. If you hadn't come up with this letter I'd have missed you, do you know that? You'd have gone back to your busy little town, to your half-hearted lover, and I'd have wondered what sort of reception I would get if I came chasing after you.'

He still had not said that he loved her, but Holly wondered whether it mattered considering all the other reasons he had put forward. She smiled tremulously. 'Aren't you afraid that I might want to change your life? Isn't that the reason you never got married?'

'It's what I told myself,' he said thickly. 'But I had never met anyone like you before. My mother tried to rule my father, in fact she made his life hell, never letting up until she got her own way. And most girls I've met never hid the fact that they were anxious to see a wedding ring on their finger. You are the only one who's ever held back.'

'I see.' Holly felt saddened by this admission. It was not the best of reasons for him wanting to marry her. No one liked to feel that they were nothing more than a challenge.

She pulled away and walked across the room, looking down into the empty fireplace, careful to keep her back to him. 'I'm sorry, Calum, I don't think I could do it.' She could not bear the thought that he might tire of her once she had given herself to him, once the novelty of having her submissive in his arms had worn off.

She heard the hiss as he took a deep breath, but he

did not come across to her. 'You're surely not going to marry Steve after all?'

'No.' She felt he deserved the truth at least.

'Then why the hell won't you marry me?' The strong tones of his voice made Holly flinch and she screwed up her face in pain, twisting her fingers nervously together.

'I can't marry without love,' she said quietly.

'My God,' he cried, 'I'll make you love me. Oh, Holly, Holly, do you think I care? I have enough love for the two of us and there's no denying that there's a chemistry between us that is really remarkable.'

He was behind her in a couple of strides, spinning her round, pulling her aggressively into his arms. Holly saw him through a blur of happy tears.

His face creased in anguish when he saw her crying. 'Is it such an impossible thing I am asking? Please, Holly, don't turn me down a second time, I don't think I could take it.'

She closed her eyes and the tears flowed even faster. 'Oh, Calum, I'm so happy. It's just the shock of—hearing you say that you love me. I never knew, truly I didn't.'

'Does that mean that you love me too?' He sounded incredulous.

Holly looked into his face and nodded, and with a groan he lowered his head, his mouth searching feverishly for hers.

Holly gave herself completely, winding her arms round his neck, desperate to reassure him of her love. The passion that raged between them was more intense than it had ever been before and when at length he lifted his head Calum's eyes were glazed with pain and desire, and Holly herself was left weak and trembling.

'You'll never know how much I needed that,' he said thickly. 'Oh, my God, Holly, let's sit down. I can't believe this is really happening.'

She nestled in the crook of his arm and decided she had never felt so warm and contented, so loved and deliriously happy. 'I do love you, Calum,' she said shyly.

'I hope you mean it,' he said with mock severity. 'I thought you did once before, when Steve came that first time, do you remember, and you refused to go back with him? I foolishly thought it was because you preferred me to him. It was distinctly humiliating to discover that it was the cottage and not me that held your interest.'

Holly smiled wryly and stroked a finger over his beautifully moulded lips. 'I made the cottage my excuse,' she said, 'even though I knew it was futile falling in love with a man who had sworn never to get married.'

'That was before I met you,' he said, taking her hand and pressing kisses into the palm. 'You went to my head the day I met you. I did not know that there were such tough independent girls about. My experience of women is that they're usually after only one thing.'

'And my experience of you is that you were after only one thing,' smiled Holly impishly.

'I was,' he said. 'You drove me crazy. I wanted you so much. I thought, that day when we went swimming, that I could teach you to love me. I set out to show you what you'd be missing if you continued your relationship with Steve. If I'd known you loved me I'd never have gone so far or been so hard on you. You must have hated me then. I'm so sorry.'

'Don't be,' whispered Holly anxiously. 'I wanted you just as much as you wanted me. All that stopped me was the fact that I thought you did not love me. It was all so wrong, so very wrong. What a couple of fools we are.'

'Not any longer, my love. We'll get married just as soon as it is humanly possible.'

He kissed her again and Holly felt as though she was transcending to another plane. How glad she was that she had met Calum before marrying Steve. She would never have known what she was missing. Perhaps Steve, too, was relieved. Perhaps he and Mandy were on this same level of happiness. She hoped so, she really did.

She hugged her love to her and knew she could afford to be magnanimous. She even felt a fleeting sadness for Duncan Gillies' carefully laid plans that had all gone wrong. It looked as though his granddaughter would have to resign herself to spinsterhood—unless he could find some other eligible bachelor who might need such a paragon of virtue as he had described. She smiled at her own thoughts.

'What is amusing you, my sweet?' asked Calum softly.

'I was wondering,' she said, 'if you might have asked Miss Drummond to marry you if I hadn't turned up.'

'Heaven forbid,' he returned strongly. 'You were my saviour, do you know that? She was Duncan's granddaughter, though he was careful not to mention it. But you couldn't mistake the relationship, they looked exactly alike.'

Holly had a quick vision of the sharp pointed nose, the cold pale eyes, and the thin legs, and she giggled.

'Definitely not your type, my darling, especially if she takes after her grandfather in his ways as well. She'd definitely rule your life.'

'How about you?' he asked softly.

She smiled into his face and kissed his mouth gently. 'I've had enough of fighting my own battles, of making my own decisions. I want to be a meek, devoted, loving, little wife.'

'Don't you dare,' he roared. 'It's your very spirit that I admire. 'Fight me, Holly, fight me every day. But love me as well. Give me your body and your soul, convince me that I've made the right decision.'

'You have, Calum, you have. I've fought you as much as I could, I've staged my own personal vendetta, but you won in the end. If that isn't true love, then I don't know what is.'

He groaned and kissed her and it was a long time before either of them moved again. Then Holly said demurely, 'Can I stay in your cottage, Calum, until we're married? I'm quite willing to pay a fair rent.'

'You little minx,' he grinned. 'I couldn't give a damn about that place. There was one time when I thought of giving it to you, but then I thought you might go away when there was nothing left to fight for.'

'I'd have still wanted to prove who truly owned it,' said Holly. 'It became an obsession.'

'And you are sorry that I was right and you were wrong?'

She smiled and shook her head. 'I was going to sell it anyway. The truth is, I only came up for one day, just to see it again, and see if there was anything of my grandparents' I wanted to keep.'

'Then you met me and changed your mind?'

'You made me see red,' confessed Holly. 'I'd never met anyone quite like you before. God, was I determined to take you down a peg or two.'

'You did,' he said humbly. 'You brought me to my knees on that very first day. I'm only sorry it's taken us so long to discover our mutual feelings.'

'The important thing,' she said, 'is that we have. If you hadn't been here when I brought my letter I'd have been on my way home now and I hate to think how long it would have been before we eventually got together again.'

'You think we would have?' he asked.

'Oh, yes,' said Holly confidently. 'When one loves as we do, it's something that's been pre-ordained, don't you think? I believe we were made for each other.'

'And these last weeks have been a testing period?' He chuckled sensuously. 'Congratulations, Miss Burns, you've passed with flying colours.'